"Oh ... ax whisp...

"I . ... d that v... e murmured, feeling the heat of his breath across her cheek.

His blue eyes were half closed, just glittering slices of indigo between thick black lashes. Even so, she saw the laughter in them. "So I lied. I need to kiss you, Jeanie. I missed you."

"You saw me five or six hours ago," she said, needing to kiss him also, but enjoying the anticipation too much to hurry. "You kissed me then. When do you get enough, Max?"

"Start kissing me and don't stop until I tell you," he said in a rough, yet quiet voice, his fingers touching each of the tiny buttons that marched down the back of her dress. He wasn't undoing them, just toying with them, maybe counting them for future reference. A delicious thrill raced down her back. "Then you'll know it's enough." His lips pressed against her palm, then nibbled the inside of her wrist. "Your eyes go all silver and shiny when I do that," he whispered huskily. "It's like smoke from a camp fire rising against a winter sky. It makes me so hot and primitive and full of wanting I could take you right here on the living-room floor."

"Max," she said, barely able to breathe. "Stop saying those things."

"Then kiss me so I can't talk. . . ."

WHAT ARE *LOVESWEPT* ROMANCES?

They are stories of true romance and touching emotion. We believe those two very important ingredients are constants in our highly sensual and very believable stories in the *LOVESWEPT* line. Our goal is to give you, the reader, stories of consistently high quality that may sometimes make you laugh, sometimes make you cry, but are always fresh and creative and contain many delightful surprises within their pages.

Most romance fans read an enormous number of books. Those they truly love, they keep. Others may be traded with friends and soon forgotten. We hope that each *LOVESWEPT* romance will be a treasure—a "keeper." We will always try to publish

LOVE STORIES YOU'LL NEVER FORGET
BY AUTHORS YOU'LL ALWAYS REMEMBER

The Editors

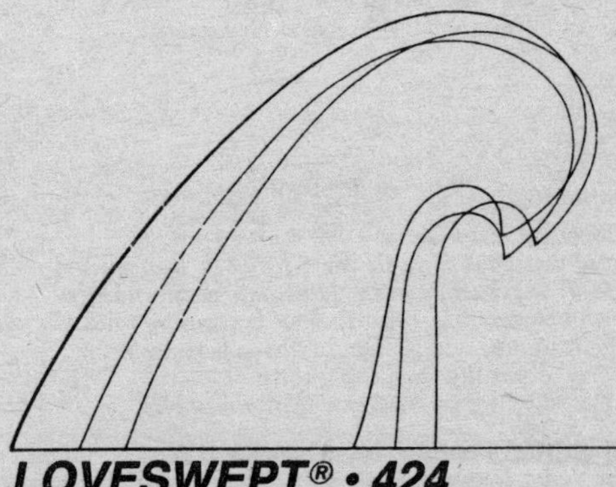

LOVESWEPT® • 424

Judy Gill

Dream Man

BANTAM BOOKS
NEW YORK • TORONTO • LONDON • SYDNEY • AUCKLAND

DREAM MAN
A Bantam Book / September 1990

LOVESWEPT® and the wave device are registered trademarks of Bantam Books, a division of Bantam Doubleday Dell Publishing Group, Inc. Registered in U.S. Patent and Trademark Office and elsewhere.

If you would be interested in receiving protective vinyl covers for your Loveswept books, please write to this address for information:

Loveswept
Bantam Books
P. O. Box 985
Hicksville, NY 11802

ISBN 0-553-44055-1

Published simultaneously in the United States and Canada

Bantam Books are published by Bantam Books, a division of Bantam Doubleday Dell Publishing Group, Inc. Its trademark, consisting of the words "Bantam Books" and the portrayal of a rooster, is Registered in U.S. Patent and Trademark Office and in other countries. Marca Registrada. Bantam Books, 666 Fifth Avenue, New York, New York 10103.

PRINTED IN THE UNITED STATES OF AMERICA

OPM 0 9 8 7 6 5 4 3 2 1

For Susan Horton,
who found me a hole in the ground,
but most of all
for Susann Brailey,
who always helps me find my way out of the holes
I dig for myself.

One

"Hey, look! Here's that nutty one again." Rolph McKenzie held the fax sheet by one corner as he walked from his office into his brother's. "I think you should go for it this time, Max."

Max laughed, shook his head, and scanned the familiar words. The ad hadn't shown up for several weeks, but there it was again. Listed under Executive Employment Opportunities, sent out on what was called the ExecNet, by J. Leslie Career Consultants, a fairly new but rapidly growing career counseling and job placement firm, the ad should have been in the Companions Wanted section of the daily paper instead.

Wanted: Tall, mature (35–45) man, heroic in nature, preferably dark haired and blue eyed, capable of making long-term commitment. Must like children, country life, and classical music. Ability to play one or more instruments an asset. Term of employment, three weekends. Apply in person to Ms. Leslie.

"Yes sir, that's some long-term commitment," Max said, laughing again.

Listening to the soft rumbling of his brother's laughter, Rolph knew the sound would have warmed any female heart—had there been a female around to hear it. That was one of Max's problems, Rolph thought. Everything about him was attractive to women. And he was one of the world's most-determined bachelors. It did create conflict in his life, having to beat them off with a bat. Rolph sighed silently. He should have such problems! All *he* attracted were "good friends" who wanted nothing more from him than to talk about his brother, maybe get a few insights, tips on how to capture the uncapturable.

Max let the paper slide onto his desk where it sat atop the messy pile of newspaper tear sheets, books and pamphlets, and scribbled notes on yellow paper. "You really think I should answer it?"

"I told you to answer it when it first appeared last month."

"And I told you then it wasn't for me."

"Yeah? Why not? It fits the only criterion you set down for researching your article: It's a weird job offer."

"Sure, but the woman is probably serious about it."

"So was the guy who advertised for an experienced pig shaver. You answered that ad, went and observed the man who was ultimately hired, and wrote a lot of good copy."

"Well, a couple of paragraphs, anyway. But this one . . ."—he shook his head—"Nah. This woman's looking for a husband. A daddy for her kids. She just hasn't got sense enough to run the ad where it would do the most good."

"Yeah, maybe. But you wouldn't have to take the job. Just go and be interviewed, ask a lot of questions, find out what it's all about."

Max nodded. "That three-weekend clause really intrigues me. I wish . . ."—he shook his head again—"Nah. It's not fair to mess with someone like that."

"You wouldn't be messing with her. You'd have no intention of taking the job. After you find out what you can about it, you prove to her somehow that you're all wrong for her, and she'll say no. Looks as if she's been doing that all along anyway, considering the number of times she ran the copy last month. And now she's started again."

"I guess you're right . . . unless she hasn't had any takers at all." Max was weakening.

"And the term of commitment is about what you usually manage," Rolph pointed out with a grin, moving the fax out of the sunlight. "You're thirty-eight, so age-wise, you qualify. Your hair is as black as coloring can make it, except at the temples where you leave that bit of silver for contrast, and your eyes are blue. You spend as much time as you can at your cabin. You've always said you'd like to raise kids if it didn't mean having to have a woman around to produce them, and you play a mean trumpet."

Max leaned back, propped his heels on the desk, linked his hands behind his head, and said, "Coloring! I oughta poke you for that one, little brother. You're the one turning gray, not me. Silver temples don't count. They merely add distinction."

"My gray hardly shows, since my hair is blond, but if I am showing my age, it's because I worry about you," said Rolph sanctimoniously. "You need some stability in your life: A wife, kiddies, lawns to mow, hedges to clip, a station wagon, a mortgage."

"Picket fences and leaky roofs, huh?" Max swung his feet to the floor, looking mildly interested. "How do you figure that as being good for me?"

"I didn't say it would be good for you to have all that. But it might be good for me."

"Then you go for it!" Max offered his brother the fax.

"What I'm saying is that it would be good for me if you got married."

Max cocked his head to one side. "Yeah? How so?"

"You're older than I am. It's time you got married. Maybe then I'd be able to get a woman to look at me for more than thirty seconds after she meets you."

"Hell." Max snorted, realizing Rolph was joking—or hoping he was. "You do okay. You just need to try harder, that's all."

"Yeah. And you don't have to try hardly at all."

Max gave his brother a sharp look, catching a pensive expression on his face. Maybe he wasn't joking? Was he still feeling sore about that bimbo who'd come on to Max so strongly a few weeks ago? Rolph hadn't been *serious* about her, had he? Max gnawed on his lower lip. Dammit, too many of Rolph's dates had deserted him, once they'd set eyes on his older brother. It had been happening virtually all their lives. They'd always joked about it. But, at thirty-six, maybe Rolph wasn't finding it funny anymore. And maybe he was right. If Max was out of the running, things might change. But, hell! He hadn't yet met the woman who turned him on so powerfully that he'd even think about marriage. He didn't believe such a woman existed. And even if she did, it wasn't up to him to run interference for his brother, was it?

". . . so why not go toot on your trumpet in front of the lonely lady and see what might fall into your lap?"

Max suddenly became aware that Rolph was speaking again. It took him a moment or two to catch up with the trend of the conversation again. "Oh!" he said when his brother's words penetrated. "The lady said 'classical,' and there ain't nothin' classical about the way I play my trumpet." He held the paper up and scanned it again, then shook his head, laying the ad on the desk. "And I'm anything but heroic. No. It's a crazy idea."

Rolph stepped into the next room, ran off a copy of the fax, picked up a highlighter, and outlined the ad in bright yellow. "There," he said, returning and dropping it onto the desk in front of his brother. "Don't lose it. I can tell you're tempted."

Max grinned. "Yeah? And how can you tell that?"

Rolph returned the grin. "You said it was a crazy idea. Are you going to have Freda phone for an appointment?"

Max slapped his palms on his desktop and stood, suddenly all business. "No. It just says 'apply in person.' And that is exactly what I'm going to do."

"Great. You do that. I'll see you when I get back from San Fran. I'll want a full report." Rolph left, chuckling and muttering to himself.

"What's that you said?" Freda, Max's research assistant looked up from her word processor. She had heard Rolph perfectly. She was only two years away from retirement, but there was nothing wrong with her hearing. It was just that it was wise to have some of the outlandish things these boys said confirmed, in case she was asked later. Once, she'd been their nanny. Then, their mother's personal assistant. Now, she worked for Max. But in reality she belonged to the whole family, and they belonged to her.

Rolph just shook his head, bent and kissed her wrinkled cheek, and said, "Forget it. Look after the idiot, Freda. See you in a week or two."

Freda nodded, brushed a lock of gray hair back from her forehead, and watched fondly as the younger McKenzie brother strode out of the huge home they shared with their parents and in which they had their offices as well. Typical McKenzie male, she thought. Long-term commitment? Three weeks? What had the boy been talking about?

"Do you have an appointment, Mr. McKenzie?" The breathless voice and the adoring expression in the eyes of the young receptionist suggested that if he didn't, she'd see to it that he soon did—with her. Their twenty-year age gap appeared to be no barrier to her.

"No, I don't, Ms. . . ."—he glanced at the nameplate on the desk—"Ms. Harrison."

"Cindy," she said, and smiled as she turned the nameplate facedown. "Ms. Harrison's away having a baby. I'm filling in. I could ask Ms. Leslie if she'd spare you five minutes. Actually, she's just on her way out for lunch, and since I know for a fact that she's lunching alone today, her client having canceled at the last minute, I'm sure—" The girl broke off as the door to the inner office opened and a tall, slender woman stepped through, then came to a dead stop, staring.

Max stared back. The woman was beautiful. Her skin was pale, iridescent gold with just a hint of peach on her cheeks. Her eyes, set wide apart and framed between thick, dark lashes, were a cool, smoky gray. As they swept over him, he believed he read fear in them, but it was so quickly masked, it was easy to persuade himself it had never been there.

Besides, why should she be afraid of him?

They had never met before; he would have remembered! And even if they had, there was nothing remotely frightening about him. As Rolph said too frequently and with unfortunate accuracy, women automatically liked him. And this person standing before him was definitely all woman. She was intensely female, even if she was trying to hide her femininity behind a tailored suit, detract from it by pulling her hair straight back, and deny it by failing to return his smile.

If this was J. Leslie, career consultant, then he was in the wrong career and needed to consult her immediately.

Jeanie stood rooted for an instant, staring at the man as if seeing a ghost—or a dream come to life. Her heart began to beat again; only then did she become aware that it had stopped for a moment or ten.

Dream men do not come to life, she told herself sternly, trying to control the wild hammering of her heart. This man's resemblance to the man she'd been dreaming about off and on for the last ten months was pure coincidence. There were plenty of tall, lean men with curly black hair and blue, blue eyes that crinkled up in a network of lines when they smiled—in women's dreams and out of them.

"Oh." The receptionist's short word brought her back to earth and suggested that only seconds had passed since she'd come through the door and seen him. Jeanie tore her gaze from the man and glanced at Cindy, who was saying, "Ms. Leslie, this is Mr. McKenzie. He doesn't have an appointment, but I was about to ask if you could spare him a few minutes."

"Uh . . ." Jeanie forced herself to look at the man again. It was no easier this time, still just as shocking to see him in person right before her. If he'd been going to come to life before anybody, then it should have been her sister Sharon. After all, it was for Sharon that she'd dreamed him up and for Sharon that she'd advertised for the man she'd seen so often in her dreams.

"Max," he said, and his voice was exactly as she'd known it would be. He extended his hand, and she took it automatically. It was warm and dry and firm and everything she had expected. She wanted to step even closer and see if he smelled the way she imagined he would. And, idiotically, she wanted just as badly to run from him, not because she had decided not to go through with her crazy plans for Sharon—which she had, weeks ago—but because seeing him there almost made her change her mind again. He was the one. He was perfect. Otherwise, why had her interfering ancestress, her father's Gypsy great-grandmother, Grandma Margaret, who was reputed to control the dreams of any of her female descendants when they were in search of a mate, put him into her dreams all those months ago? It was ridiculous! Sharon was the one supposed to have inherited all the Gypsy blood, along with the big dark eyes and the sleek black hair. Jeanie had no Gypsy characteristics, and the fact that she had been doing the dreaming about this man had no bearing on anything, she told herself. Maybe Grandma Margaret's powers were weakening, and she'd screwed up, put the dreams into the wrong sister's head. It was Sharon who wanted a husband, not Jeanie!

The practicality she'd inherited from her mother's side of the family told her that she had held the man's hand quite long enough. She pulled free, but she saw in his eyes his reluctance to let her go. Because she prided herself on being sensible, she ignored his look.

"Just a few minutes of your time?" he asked in that soft, velvety voice that wrapped itself around her heart and warmed her from the inside out. Oh, yes! He'd make the ideal . . . brother-in-law . . . if she'd still been searching for a man for her sister. But she was not! And she had never been searching for one for herself.

"No," she said, hoping he wouldn't guess that the high-pitched, ragged tone was not her normal speaking voice. "I don't have time right now. I'm meeting someone for lunch." *Grandma Margaret, why are you tempting me this way?*

"But she canceled," said Cindy. "Remember? I told you just a few minutes ago that Mrs. Anthony wouldn't be able to make it and—" As if finally noticing her employer's eloquent stare, she said,

"I'm sorry, Ms. Leslie. Me and my big mouth, huh?"

"Yes, Cindy." Jeanie sighed, then smiled ruefully at the girl's flushed, guilty face. "I know you try hard." She also suspected that her pesky ancestress might have put the words into the girl's mouth. She switched her slatey gaze to Max. Was this destiny speaking, after all? Was Somebody up there other than Grandma Margaret telling her to go with her first instincts and take this man to Sharon against all better judgment? What should she do? If he was the answer to Sharon's needs, did she have the right to refuse to hear what he had to say? After all, because she didn't really believe in any old Gypsy predictions and superstitions, her own must be the mind that had conjured him up in the first place. Maybe she should get to know him a little bit, see what he was all about, before she made a firm decision. She drew in a deep breath and nodded. "All right, then, Mr. McKenzie. Please come in. I can spare you a few minutes."

"Max," he corrected her once more. "Maybe we could talk over lunch," he suggested.

She froze inside. Would that be wise? No! Absolutely not. "No, thank you. I prefer to conduct business in my office," she said pleasantly. Why he had come, why he wanted to see her, she had no idea, but she doubted it was to tell her that he'd been dreaming about a woman who looked exactly like Sharon for most of the past year. She doubted just as strongly that he was there to tell her that he wanted to meet her sister and bring her out of her depression, to make her into a whole and happy human once again, to become the father Jason and Roxanne needed. But whatever it was he wanted from her, she'd feel safer hearing it with the barrier of her big oak desk between them. She flicked another glance at him and he smiled a smile she was utterly powerless to resist. She thought for a crazy moment that if he'd held out his arms to her just then, she'd have walked right into them.

"Since you were on your way out to lunch, obviously you need to eat. So do I. Wouldn't it be so much easier and save time, if we did it together?" he asked.

Jeanie hesitated. The man's logic was undeniable. She had to eat. She had a table booked already. And she was a big girl, thirty-one years old. She could look after herself, and maybe she'd learn more about him in a less formal atmosphere than her office. She knew she should be as nice to him as possible. After all, she mustn't forget that someone looking just like Max McKenzie had been peopling her dreams, filling her with the certainty that somewhere, sometime she'd find him, and he'd put Sharon's world back together again the way she and all the king's horses hadn't been able to do.

Suddenly, she knew she had no choice. If he wanted to have lunch with her, then that was what would happen. Maybe Grandma Margaret *was* in charge of her mind and events. "All right, Mr. McKenzie," she said. "I can spare you an hour, but no more. This way, please."

She held the door open for him. Behind them, the receptionist said wistfully, "Have a nice lunch, Ms. Leslie. And don't hurry. Remember, you have no more appointments today."

"An hour, huh? No more?"

Jeanie had to laugh as she led her companion

past the elevator doors and toward the stairs. "Cindy is a temporary maternity-leave replacement," she said. "But the girl does try very hard. It's just that she's young and impulsive and says anything that comes into her head. I hope to teach her some discretion."

"I'm sure time will, if you don't," he said easily as they started down the four flights of stairs. "The elevator worked fine when I came up a few minutes ago."

"Did it?" she asked. "Exercise is good for you, Mr. McKenzie."

"Max," he said, taking her arm, dragging in deep breaths of the delicate scent that wafted up from her hair.

"I beg your pardon?" she asked as if she hadn't heard him.

"My name is Max." He wanted to hear her say his name in that sexy, husky voice of hers. Never had he wanted so much to hear a woman say his name, but she seemed determined to be all business.

"Yes, I know." She slipped her arm out of his clasp, swung her shoulder bag in between them, and returned his warm smile with a small, cool one of her own. She was, he realized with a slight sense of shock and a large dose of curiosity, completely impervious to that so-called natural charm his brother envied. Why? When his body chemistry reacted so wildly to her, wasn't the feeling supposed to be mutual? She was also, he realized, not going to offer her first name in response to his.

"My car's just around the corner," he said as they came down the last flight of stairs and into the building's lobby.

"Mine's right out here," said Jeanie, pushing open the door to the staff parking area at the rear of the building, stepping out into a swirl of golden leaves from the autumn-gold poplars between the lot and the sidewalk. Dream man or not, she wasn't getting into a car with a man she had never met before and knew absolutely nothing about. Not unless she was behind the wheel and in control.

Sharon had taught her that much—and considerably more, Jeanie mused as she drove through the crowded streets of downtown Victoria. It hadn't been easy for Sharon, at eighteen years old, to take up the rearing of a little sister. In a small apartment in downtown Toronto, all the two girls could afford while Sharon attended the Royal Conservatory of Music after their parents had died, she and her sister had survived some rough times together.

Her passenger broke into her thoughts. "Nice car. I've always admired Hondas."

"Thank you. I find it comfortable to drive."

"Yes. I can tell. You're a very smooth driver." She glanced at him, pleased with the comment, but did not reply. She felt vaguely surprised to learn that he wasn't one of those dinosaurs who hated to have a woman drive him. Sneakily, she watched from the corner of her eye as he sat back, his gaze switching from small glances at her face to the passing scenes of Government Street. When she parked the car, he was out his door and around to her side in a few long-legged paces. He opened her door and helped her out, his hand large and warm on her elbow. As she had on the stairs, she pulled away quickly. She was determined to keep this luncheon on a businesslike plane, especially because the mere touch of his hand had the extraordinary ability to turn her insides to butterscotch pudding. Things like this did not happen to Jeanie Leslie.

When they were seated, had been served coffee, and their orders had been taken, she leaned back in her chair and smiled, hoping her professional calm properly masked her deepening interest in him.

Who was he? Had she seen him somewhere before? She had an active social life. Maybe they'd attended the same party once or twice, she'd seen him across the room and had subconsciously remembered him. That could account for his having figured so largely in her dreams these last months. But even as she thought it, she knew she was trying to fool herself. If she'd seen Max McKenzie, even across a crowded room, she'd have remembered with more than her subconscious. Extreme caution was called for here, she thought. Maybe even a little chicken-hearted cowardice.

"Now, Mr. McKenzie," she said briskly, wanting to get this meeting over with fast, "how can I help you?"

He considered telling her, but it was far too soon in their relationship for him to say what was uppermost in his mind, that his brother had given him the germ of an idea, and meeting her had given that little seed a helluva big dose of growth hormone. Besides, he was certain that if he gave himself a day or two to reflect, he'd realize the idea was one of the dumbest he'd ever entertained. So what if she was the most beautiful creature he'd ever seen, with her pink and gold skin, tawny-colored hair, smoky eyes? So what if the scent she exuded made his head reel? So what if she walked as if she wore a tiara and long, ermine-trimmed robes? So what if he had, for one wild moment, suddenly felt as though there might be such a thing as love at first sight? It was impossible, because love itself was impossible. No, this was purely the worst case of lust he'd ever suffered, exacerbated by her failure to respond to him as women always did. Some devil in him demanded that he break through that cool reserve of hers, make those smoky eyes flare with flames of excitement. Ah, yes. Good, old-fashioned lust. There was nothing to do but wait it out. It would go away in time, especially if he didn't see her again. He remembered once when he was in college he'd gotten so dizzy over the sight and scent of a flight attendant that he'd wanted to ask for oxygen. At least the experience had proven to him that he was capable of going off the deep end momentarily, but that it would also pass. So he said what he'd come to say before he'd had it wiped from his mind by the sight of her tall slender body and fantastic gray eyes.

"You can start by telling me your first name."

"Jeanie." She gave a tiny shrug, more impressed than she liked to admit when he didn't automatically respond with the usual, ". . . with the light brown hair."

"I'd like to know more about the job that requires a mature man who likes children, country life, and classical music, Jeanie."

To his surprise, her cool facade broke for an instant, and her eyes flared not with excitement or pleasure but with that hint of fear he'd seen before.

She stared at him, reared back slightly in her chair, and said sharply, "No! Absolutely not."

Two

Jeanie felt her mind go blank for a moment, then fill with tangled thoughts. She had known. On the most basic of levels, she had known the moment she saw him that he had come to her for one reason only, weeks late, maybe, but who was she to argue with destiny? Except that now she found she didn't want him to know she had placed that ad personally, or why. What held her back she couldn't say, but maybe it was because he was *so* right it terrified her. But she realized Sharon would never be able to handle a man like him, not in her present state of mind. He was too strong, too overwhelming. Too . . . male.

"No!" she said, shocked to hear the incipient panic in her voice. She shook her head to clear it, forced the fear down, and brought herself under tight control. "I'm sorry," she said pleasantly, but firmly, keeping her gaze on his face, "but that job isn't being offered any longer."

"Oh?" His brows lifted. "It came over the Exec-Net this morning on my brother's fax machine."

"It did?" Her shock was evident again, but she controlled it even more quickly than before. "If so, then it was sent out by mistake." She pulled a wry face and sighed dramatically, rolling those gorgeous gray eyes heavenward.

He smiled. "Cindy?"

With a small laugh, she nodded. "I guess so. Poor Cindy."

"Why not poor you? You have to put up with her."

She gave him a level stare. "I do not *have* to put up with her. I choose to. If you had ever been a young woman looking for office work, you'd understand why. So many ads read, Junior office clerk wanted. Must have at least two years' experience. And then they offer a rate of pay so insultingly low that no male would ever be expected to live on it. I used to wonder how and where young women were supposed to gain experience if no one would hire them until they had some. So I take them on right out of school and train them whenever I get a chance and encourage my clients to do the same."

He smiled and reached across the table to touch the back of her left hand, drawing a blunt, white nail from the base of her ring finger to the tip. "You're a nice woman, Jeanie Leslie."

She withdrew her hand slowly and looked at him, wondering why she was so fierce in her determination to keep Max and Sharon apart. She didn't usually feel quite so strongly about things of this nature. She was being protective, that was all. She dragged her mind back to their conversation. "Thank you. But I don't do it to be nice. I do it because it's right."

He startled her with his next question. "Are you a single mother?"

She blinked, and he saw again how long and thick and black her lashes were. Incredible!

"Why, no!" she said, surprised. "I'm not a mother. Why do you ask?"

"Because of the ad."

She turned a delicate shade of pink but met his gaze steadily. "That ad," she said crisply, "was withdrawn several weeks ago."

"Why?"

She stared at him. "Why? Mr. McKenzie, an advertisement can be dropped at any time. A person can change her mind about her . . . requirements."

"I'm aware of that," he said with the same easy grace he'd shown when he'd accepted her decision to take her car. His eyes danced, she thought, with slightly mocking humor. "How long after I walked through that door did you change your mind about your requirements?"

"What?"

"I said—"

"I heard the words, Mr. McKenzie. It was their meaning I was questioning." Her voice was cold.

"Ms. Leslie . . . Jeanie, you sent out that particular ad." It was not a question.

"Yes, I did. Originally. But not today. Sending out advertisements is one of my functions as a career consultant. I help place clients who are seeking employment with those who are seeking employees, and vice versa. I try to match the right person with the right company."

"Exactly. But clearly, it was not a company requiring a mature man who likes children and music and capable of forming a long-term attachment, or words to that effect. It was a woman."

Jeanie barely resisted the urge to shift in her chair, to look away from him, to gnaw on her lip. Any of those actions would have been completely unprofessional and would have shown the agitation she was feeling. "It was," she stated. "But I assure you, I am not the woman who was searching for a . . . mate. I simply placed the ad. However, details of any contract I might have with a client are confidential. And since, as I mentioned, the ad has been withdrawn, I see no need to discuss it. Who do you think will win the Grey Cup this year, Mr. McKenzie?"

He laughed. "You placed that ad. And I don't think it was for a client. Again I ask why?"

What right did he have to be so damned perceptive? Did he have a Gypsy great-great-grandmother somewhere in his background too? She assumed her most professional demeanor. "And again I must point out that I am under no obligation to tell you why or whom or what or anything further about it. And I resent your harping on it, Mr. McKenzie."

He looked contrite. "I'm sorry. Perhaps you'd let me explain?"

"Why don't you?" she agreed. "Tell me what makes a man like you apply for such a job."

He leaned back as the waiter set her salad before her and his clam chowder before him. Picking up his spoon, he said, "A man like me?"

For just a second, he thought he detected chagrin in her expression, but she quickly and successfully masked it. Damn! Would he ever be able to read her successfully? And why was it so important that he be able to? After he found out about that dumb job offer, he wasn't going to see her again. Was he?

"Surely," she said, "you have no difficulty in finding women. You're not ugly, I haven't noticed that you smell bad, and you have a pleasant manner. Most of the time."

He smiled. "Did you expect to get ugly, unpleasant, and smelly applicants, Ms. Leslie?"

To his delight, she laughed and her eyes lightened. "Touché, Mr. McKenzie."

"Max. And I came to discuss that ad because I'm a free-lance writer."

"Ahh . . ." Sympathy and understanding flashed across her face. He realized she thought he had foolishly and prematurely given up his day job.

"No, it's not like that," he said with a laugh. "I don't need extra work. In fact, I don't want the job you offered at all."

She was incapable of replying. He didn't want to meet Sharon? He wasn't interested in being a hero like the one she'd dreamed up, ready and eager to rescue her sister from all manner of perils? He wasn't looking for a wife? She didn't know which emotion was uppermost, relief or disappointment. She could only stare at him, feeling buffeted by winds of doubt and confusion. *She* had changed her mind, dammit! She had withdrawn the ad! Why should she feel so let down to know that he wasn't interested in the position?

After a moment, she said, "Fine. Then there's nothing to discuss, is there? There's no job, and if there were, you wouldn't want it. What's your favorite vacation spot, Mr. McKenzie?"

"It's true I'm not applying for the job." He smiled. "If there were a job. And call me Max."

"Of course. If." Her tone was as dry as his had been, but her gray eyes sparkled with sudden, silent laughter. She did not call him Max.

"But I do want to know about it," he went on as if she hadn't interrupted. "I'm doing an article on strange jobs and intriguing job offers. And," he added with a smile, "you must surely admit that a job description calling for someone capable of making a long-term commitment, then saying that the length of employment would be three weekends, certainly qualifies as odd."

"Well, yes, I suppose it does." Her voice sounded rough edged. She cleared her throat and said, "It's an interesting idea, that article of yours. How long have you been working on it? Have you always been a writer? What other strange job offers have you researched so far?"

She knew she was talking too much, that she wasn't giving the man a chance to answer. She drew in a deep breath and let it out slowly, then forced herself to pick up her fork and start in on her turkey salad.

"Chicken catching, for one," he said, his gaze still on her face.

"What?" She laughed, realizing that his intent gaze no longer made her quite so uncomfortable. It probably was just the way he looked at everyone. Maybe she was getting used to it. She hoped so. She wanted to get used to it. To him. She wanted to be able to get tired of him. To be able to turn her back on him, forget her erstwhile plans for Sharon. Maybe now that she'd met him, he'd get out of her dreams. She ate some more, while he spooned up his thick chowder and broke a piece off the small hot loaf in a basket between them. He offered her some, but she shook her head and slid the dish of butter curls closer to him.

"Someone hires people to catch chickens?" she asked. "And what do you do with them once you've caught them?"

"Stuff them into cages so they can be taken to market. It pays surprisingly well, but the chicken growers over in Fraser Valley still have a hard time keeping competent staff."

"Why is that?"

He wrinkled his nose as if remembering. "It's a lousy job."

That piqued her interest. "Did you actually do it? Do you take on every job you want to learn about?" Was he willing to go and meet Sharon? At that very moment she realized she did not want him to meet her sister—because she wanted him all to herself. The realization was so startling, she scarcely heard his next words and had to force herself to concentrate on what he was saying.

He shook his head. "Not every one, but that one I did for two nights. Just for the experience. It has to be done at night, of course, because the chickens are slow and stupid with sleep."

She laughed softly again. "I thought chickens were slow and stupid at the best of times." Of course he wouldn't want to meet a woman "just for the experience." She knew a nice man when she met one.

"Probably are, but they're more-so at night. I can understand why it's hard to keep staff, though. You grab the birds by their feet, two in each hand, and stuff them into wire cages, all the while trying to keep the ones you've already crammed in there from getting out again. It's a messy, smelly job, and the damn things squawk and flap and try to get away."

She had to say something to hide the crazy spinning of her mind. She had to appear normal and rational and intelligent. She laughed lightly again and said, "Well, really, do you blame them, Max?"

He could only stare at her, wordless. She had said his name. At last, she had said it. And it had sounded as good as he'd thought it would, soft and warm and husky. He wanted to ask her to whisper it. He wanted what? Was he out of his everlovin' mind? He pondered that idea. Maybe he was. Maybe that would account for the odd things happening to him, the odd notions that had kept popping into his head ever since he'd set eyes on Jeanie Leslie. He smiled into her gray eyes, thinking about how his name had sounded on her lips. For some reason he couldn't think about anything else.

Jeanie was lost in the intensity of his stare for several minutes before she gave herself a mental shake and took another mouthful of broken lettuce. She chewed it, swallowed, then pushed her plate away. She'd never much cared for cardboard with oil and vinegar dressing. She leaned forward slightly, elbows on the table as she pulled her coffee cup toward her, wishing Max McKenzie would quit looking at her like that, that he'd say something, anything, to break the sudden tension between them.

Max swallowed hard as he saw the front of her suit jacket gape slightly, revealing the curve of her breasts under her pink silk blouse, a vee of delicate skin, the fine gold chain that disappeared down under her blouse. He wanted to follow that chain and see where it went. He wanted to—

He forced himself to lift his gaze back to her face. Jeanie Leslie was too much a lady to like being ogled in public. He didn't know how he knew that or why he'd let it stop him, but in the past half hour he hadn't seemed to be too smart at all. About anything.

"Max? Are you all right?" Her voice, saying his name again, came from far away. He had to look down so she wouldn't see in his eyes the surge of lust that rose in his body.

"Mmm–hmm." His reply was just a rumble of sound, no words. He stared at the table as intently as he'd stared at her. Jeanie felt relieved. More or less. So she'd been right. He did look at everyone the same way. Even tables.

"Well, do you?" she prompted him when he remained silent.

He lifted his gaze to her face once again, and she saw that his eyes were expressionless.

"Do I what?" he asked.

"Blame them."

"Blame who?"

"The chickens."

"For what?"

She frowned. What was wrong with him all of a sudden? Was he bored with this conversation? Probably. It was pretty inane. But it was his work they were talking about, for heaven's sake. "For trying to get away," she said patiently.

"Oh." He blinked and seemed to come back from wherever it was his mind had drifted to. "Yes. Of course." He smiled and his eyes came to life again. "I mean, no, of course I don't blame them. I'd flap and squawk, too, if anyone ever tried to stuff me into a cage." Something compelled him to add with deadly seriousness, "I hate cages."

There was a moment's silence during which their smiles faded and their gazes met in grave contemplation of his words, and then she nodded. "Yes. I do too."

It was true. She had always avoided relationships that might have led to something permanent. She'd told herself it was because she'd wanted a business of her own and had been working hard to create one. The couple of men she might have made a life with had wanted her to be someone else, and she'd had enough grief watching Sharon try to change to ever want to do it herself.

Maybe that was a cage of sorts, but it was one of her own making, and it wasn't the kind of cage she and Max McKenzie had both tacitly referred to. She was glad they had both laid those cards on the table. She was aware of his interest in her and knew he was male enough to read her responses. Her initial interest in him had been purely for her sister's benefit. His initial interest in her had been because of that ridiculous ad. Any further curiosity they might be feeling toward each other was going to have to be curbed after their luncheon was over. But it wouldn't hurt to enjoy this short time in his company, she decided.

"What . . . what other strange jobs have you researched so far?" she said, caught up in a need to fill the heavy silence.

"Oh . . . pig shaving." He appeared startled by her question. "Someone advertised for an experienced pig shaver. That one caught my attention."

Jeanie lifted her elbows and sat back so the waiter could refill her coffee cup. When he had topped off Max's as well, she asked, "And did you take that job for the experience too?"

He shook his head. One black curl fell forward on his brow. He shoved it back absently. Her fingertips tingled. Her insides quivered. She frowned and made a fist in her lap, pressing it against her lower abdomen where the quiver had been worst.

"When a job calls for experience I don't have, I level with the employer, explain what it is I'm doing, and sometimes get permission to observe the one who is hired. The chicken-catching position didn't demand experience, so I gave it a try."

"What does a pig shaver do? I mean, I realize it sounds pretty self-explanatory, but how do you get the pig to stand still, and why would anybody want one shaved?"

"Dead pigs don't wiggle," he said, and for some reason, maybe his deadpan delivery, her laughter gurgled up and floated around him, taking his breath away, delighting him with its beauty. He scowled for a moment. He was getting far too interested in this woman for his own good. Women came on to Max McKenzie. He did not come on to women. He didn't have to. There was no conceit in the knowledge, just an acceptance of facts. And regardless of what Rolph had suggested, he had no intention of putting himself out of circulation, because there were times when he enjoyed his easy popularity with the opposite sex. Getting interested in one specific woman, getting tied up in any permanent, legal way would not just curtail that, it would stop it in its tracks.

"Dead pigs don't wiggle," she said. "Sounds like

the title of a bad mystery novel. Do you write fiction, too, Max?"

"No," he said, "not so far, anyway." Then, after pouring several envelopes of sugar into his coffee and stirring briskly for several moments, he looked up and caught her gaze on his face.

"Tell me," he said, leaning back and looking at her quizzically. "With that ad, and the way it was phrased, to say nothing of your placing it on the ExecNet instead of in the classifieds of the daily papers, did you have any takers at all?"

She sighed. He was determined to talk about the ad, wasn't he? Did he always get his own way? Probably, she realized. With those eyes and that smile, almost assuredly. "Yes," she said resignedly. Why not tell him a little about it, just to help him with his research? Maybe then he'd drop the subject. "I—we—got more than a dozen the first week we ran it; after that, it tapered off a bit, but it still garnered responses every time I sent it out."

"You ran it weekly. None of the candidates were suitable?"

"She chuckled. "Wildly unsuitable, if you want the truth, though not one actually smelled bad."

"Maybe you got unsuitable candidates because of where you placed the ad. I wondered what your reasoning was, there. I mean, the personals would have seemed more appropriate."

"No." She shook her head and a fine halo of curly, light brown hair that had sprung free from her severe style caught the sunlight behind her, outlining her face with a golden glow. He immediately remembered the Christmas tree angel in his grandmother's home. "I deliberately didn't put it in the Companions Wanted section of the newspaper, because it was to be a paid position, and I thought executives looking for other employment might be intrigued enough by the phrasing to reply."

He laughed. "Oh, you got that right! It drove my brother, Rolph, crazy. He subscribes to ExecNet because he's expanding his boat brokerage firm and is on the lookout for just the right man for the number two spot."

Jeanie lifted her brows. "Or woman, I hope," she said dryly.

"Oh, yes. Of course." That idea, in itself was novel. Had Rolph ever considered a woman as second in command? He had to laugh silently at the idea. As much as Rolph liked women, had more women as good friends than he really wanted, he also had definite ideas about women in positions of power. Women, as far as Rolph was concerned, should be lilies of the field.

"Anyway," he went on, "Rolph's the one who prodded me to reply when your ad came out again today. Tell me, if you can without breaking any confidences, do you—does your client, rather—really believe that three weekends constitutes a long-term commitment?"

Again, she laughed. Again, he felt the magic of it wrap itself around him. He swallowed hard. This was not the way it was supposed to happen. He was thirty-eight years old, and he hadn't felt this way in the presence of a woman for more than twenty years! He had to stop his libido from getting out of control. It was as simple as that. Except, where Jeanie Leslie was concerned, controlling his libido wasn't simple. It reminded him of a game they used to play with a greased watermelon in the lake as kids. The minute you thought you had a grip on it, it went slipping and sliding and bobbing away completely out of your command.

"Of course not," she said, replying to his question and snatching his attention back where it belonged—on their conversation and off her incredible, sexy charm. "But three weekends was all I—we—were willing to pay for. If the man we chose hadn't decided by then that he wanted to see my . . . client again without being paid, he wasn't the right one. At least, that was the theory. I admit it was an ill-conceived idea and one I was glad to drop."

"Did the client ever find someone who suited her?"

Jeanie shook her head. "No. In fact, she never even met any of the candidates. I was in charge of . . . selection. And none of them was even remotely possible."

"What do you think accounts for that?"

None of them looked like you. She sighed and shrugged. "I'm not sure. Probably, as I said, because it was a stupid idea to begin with. None of them was acceptable because the entire idea was ill-conceived. No matter how desperate the situation, no one has the right or the ability to choose a potential mate for anyone else."

This man was wanted to alleviate a "desperate situation"? The whole thing grew more and more intriguing. "Then why wasn't the client in charge of selection?"

Her arched brows drew together and she caught her full lower lip in her white teeth. A shiver ran up Max's arms, across his chest, and down his belly, tightening muscles as it went. Painfully.

"I'm sorry. As I said earlier, that was a confidential matter and I don't care to discuss it further. I think I've told you enough. You can use what little I've been able to tell you, if you'd find it helpful, but no more details." She glanced at her watch and shoved her chair back. "And now, I have to get back to work. My lack of appointments doesn't necessarily mean I have no jobs to do this afternoon. I'll drop you back at your car." She deftly picked up the little tray with the tab on it, handed him one of the two mints, and slipped out from behind the table.

"Excuse me," he said, taking the tray from her hand, "but I invited you."

She smiled coolly and slid past him. "Did you?" she asked. "Yes, I suppose you did. But since you didn't get what you wanted from our meeting, I'd be happy to stand you lunch."

He looked at her intently. "Didn't I get what I wanted, Jeanie? Maybe not this time. But I will."

What does he mean? she wondered.

"I'll meet you at the car," she said quietly as he turned to the cashier and she to the door.

Three

"I'm sure that's not the only strange ad you've ever had to run on behalf of a client," he said as they drove back toward her office building. "Would you be willing to share some others with me—without breaking professional codes of ethics, of course—if you think of any?"

She didn't want to be tempted with an excuse to see him again. "No. I don't often get odd requests like that. Not as a rule." Of course she didn't. Most people had far more sense than she had shown in conceiving the idea in the first place. Most people discounted dreams, even recurring ones. "This is a pretty straightforward business. Maybe you could try some of the other agencies."

"Aren't they 'straightforward'?"

She flicked a glance at him and caught sight of his incredible smile again. Every little part of her responded to it. It made her mad even while it excited her so much, she almost drove into the back of a bus. It wasn't fair! No woman should have to try to drive sensibly with a man like Max McKenzie smiling at her from the passenger seat. Maybe if she stopped, told him to get into the backseat and crouch down so she couldn't see him, they'd both be safer. Except then he'd know how crazy he was making her.

"Of course they're straightforward," she said. "What I meant was, if you spread the word around about what you're looking for, maybe you'll have better results. No point in relying on one source."

"I won't. But if you do find something you think might be right for me, will you call?" He reached into his breast pocket and took out a card, placing it on the dash just as she swung the car into the parking lot behind her building.

She stared at the little white rectangle as she pulled up on the hand brake and turned off the ignition. Then, almost against her will, she reached out and took it, dropping it into an outside pocket of her purse.

"Yes," she said. "Of course, Mr. McKenzie."

"Hey," he said, "you called me Max just a few minutes ago. Why the return to formality?"

Jeanie opened her door, stepped out and looked at him across the car roof when he had alighted. "Good-bye, Mr. McKenzie. Thank you for the lunch." She couldn't begin to explain to him why she felt the need to hide behind what he called formality. She couldn't even explain it to herself. But she felt it was better that they stay several arm's lengths away from each other even when they were saying good-bye. And why not be formal? It wasn't as though she intended to see him again.

He didn't stay several arm's lengths away, or

even one car width. He came right up to her, smiled at her, bent his head, and brushed an impudent kiss over her lips. Then, lifting his hand in a little salute, he said, "See you, Jeanie," then strode away along the sidewalk and around the corner, out of sight.

Jeanie stood there for several minutes, gripping her purse so tightly, her hands ached. Her insides shook. Her head spun. Her knees knocked. She would not, under any circumstances, see that man again. She wondered bleakly as she climbed the four flights of stairs to her office if there were some way she could ensure that she would never go to sleep again. Because if she did, she knew she would see him—in her dreams.

"It's not fair! It simply is not fair."

"Did you call me, Ms. Leslie?"

Jeanie looked up. "No, Cindy. I was talking to myself. It's all right. Go on home now. It's late."

"Yes, ma'am. I was just going."

Jeanie scarcely heard the younger woman. She sat with her hands in her hair, staring at the letter before her. Talk about an odd job request! And why had it been sent to her, of all people? Was it to tempt her? She lifted her head and gazed at the ceiling. "Grandma Margaret, is this your doing?"

Nothing. No response of any kind. Well, she hadn't expected one, had she? She didn't really believe that she'd inherited any of Grandma Margaret's Gypsy characteristics. If anything, she'd inherited something far more valuable: Her own mother's practical streak. And it was that very practicality that had made her file Max McKenzie's business card instead of tossing it in the garbage as she probably should have a week ago. She never threw out anything like that, just in case she might need it one day, and dammit, this was the day she would have to call him.

She wracked her brains. Did she know of any other free-lance writer who might be capable of coming up with what the client wanted in the time he wanted it? Did she know any other writers at all? Unfortunately, no. She frowned as she got to her feet and strode to a bookcase on the far side of her office.

Taking down a folder from a shelf, Jeanie opened it to the "Mac" section and there it lay, tucked into its little plastic pocket. Max McKenzie's card. Although it was plain white and not at all fancy, it still had a look of understated elegance about it. Old money, or something. Slightly raised black letters and numbers formed his name, telephone number, and the address to which she'd sent the brief and polite thank-you note after his unostentatious but beautiful floral arrangement had arrived the day after their lunch. Of course, the fact that it was a Beacon Hill address had certainly added to the impression of old money.

But for this, a note wouldn't do. She had to call him. She marched back to her desk and sat down. With her hand on the phone, she closed the folder and rehearsed what she would say. When the phone rang right under her palm, she leapt about two feet out of her chair, her eyes so wide her eyeballs nearly fell out, and every hair stood on end.

"Jeanie Leslie," she said into the phone.

* * *

A few moments after leaving Jeanie Leslie in the parking area at the rear of her building, Max had convinced himself quite firmly that he was fully in control, not only of his libido, but of his future, and that she, as lovely as she was, had absolutely no part in it. The next morning, after a night of pursuing her through his dreams, he was less convinced but determinedly put her out of his mind, concentrating instead on one of the articles he was currently working on—but not the one dealing with strange job offers.

By noon, he was ready to tear his hair out. She would not stay out of his mind. He remembered her scent. He heard over and over her husky, soft voice speaking his name. What would it be like to hear it again? He stared at the phone, then looked resolutely away. No, dammit, she had made it clear that she didn't want anything more to do with him. There were plenty of women in the world who did want him. More than he cared to count. He took his personal phone directory and opened it at random, lifted the phone, and began to punch in numbers. There was that red-head who lived over in Saanich. She'd always been ready for anything. Hearing the splatter of rain against his window, he remembered she was spending the wet season in Palm Springs. He set the phone down.

The next name that leapt out at him was that of a rather sweet woman who claimed quite openly to be in love with him. He'd stopped seeing her because it wasn't fair to give her hope for anything more than friendship. Still, her adulation had been damned good for the ego, and

Jeanie Leslie, with her obvious immunity to him, had certainly not been. Lifting the phone again, he dialed the florist his family had dealt with for years, ordered an arrangement sent to Jeanie at her office, dictated a brief note of thanks for her help on his article, and decided that would be that.

And later he had gone upstairs and dreamed again of Jeanie Leslie.

It wasn't fair, he decided a week later. He picked up the phone, punched in numbers he had no need to look up, and was startled to hear her answer before even half a ring had sounded in his ear.

Jeanie nearly slammed the phone down when Max McKenzie said, "Hello, Jeanie Leslie," in that voice that did things to her traitorous insides. "This is Max McKenzie. I know it's short notice, but are you free for dinner tonight?"

Her heart slammed hard inside her ribs, once, twice, then slowed to a regular beat as her eyes rolled heavenward, and she slumped back in her chair, suddenly resigned. Only . . . resignation didn't usually feel like this, did it? All tingling tummy, flighty head, and curving smile that just would not quit no matter how hard she tried?

"I . . . uh, yes, as a matter of fact, I am," she said, careful to keep her voice calm and contained. *All right, Grandma Margaret. Why don't you let me in on what's happening before it happens? Isn't there some kind of sign you could have sent me before you sicced the man on me again?*

"Great!" He sounded as if he really meant it.

Inside her, something fluttered like one of his chickens getting shoved into a cage. But it didn't squawk even a tiny bit in protest, she noticed. "Eight o'clock? May I have your address so I can pick you up?"

Jeanie bit her lip. Like getting into a car with a strange man, giving out her address to someone she didn't know was something Sharon had warned her against over and over. Once, she had thought her sister was unduly cautious, but the older she grew, the more she became aware of the things that could happen. And she had to admit that being responsible for the care and well-being of three other people tended to make her less intrepid than she had once been. "I'd rather meet you somewhere."

In a puzzled tone he said, "All right. If that's what you prefer." He named the restaurant where he would book a table, and Jeanie hung up, watching as her hand trembled on the pale blue phone.

At home, she dressed in a cowl-necked green silk dress, looked at herself in the full-length mirror in her bedroom, shook her head, and muttered, "No." The dark brown velvet skirt and cream silk blouse she tried next weren't right, either. They joined the green silk dress on the bed. After three more attempts, she went back to the brown velvet skirt, but teamed it with a pale primrose angora sweater with satin and gold bead applique. Then she fixed earrings of gold and enamel to her lobes, and added six fine gold bangles to her right wrist—the jewelry all heirlooms from Grandma Margaret—tamed her hair with two combs that matched the earrings, and with a quick spritz of perfume, was ready. She glanced out the window, noting that it was still raining, and added a good coat of hair spray to keep the kinks at bay.

Maybe, she thought in disgust ten minutes later, feeling the frizz start to puff out around her temples as she got into her car, she should consider moving to New Mexico or the Sahara desert. Would her hair then be sleek and manageable like Sharon's? Oh, dammit, why did it have to matter so much how she looked for Max McKenzie? She was seeing him tonight for one reason only: To tell him about that job. This was not a date in the usual sense. At least, not on her part. She experienced a moment's light-headedness as she realized that he had never said exactly why he had called her.

Did he think of it as a date?

And if he did, what did it mean to him?

And even more to the point, what did it mean to her?

Jeanie drove by the restaurant. Both sides of the street were filled with cars; every parking meter taken in a three-block radius. Slowly, she circled several blocks looking for a spot that was close to the restaurant so she wouldn't have to walk too far in the rain, but her luck failed to improve. With a grimace, she drove into a parking garage and circled up, up, and up some more, before finding a small slot she could just manage to shoehorn her car into.

Grabbing her keys and umbrella, she slid out of the car and looked around. Cold, damp, lonely garages were not among her favorite places, and the sooner she got out of this one, the better. Quickly, she walked to the stairs, aware of the way the heels of her shoes rang out on the concrete, saying, "Woman alone, woman alone, woman alone . . ." *Oh, quit being paranoid,* she told herself as she headed for the red-painted metal stairwell door. She changed her pace, causing her heels to ring out, "I'm tough! I'm tough! I'm tough!" instead.

She laughed aloud at her own bravado and reached out to push open the stairwell door. Her laughter died into a rattling gasp that caught in her throat as a large, dirty hand closed over her wrist, jerking her away from the door. The man, nothing more than a large, dark shape from the shadows, tugged on her, pulling her off balance, swinging her into the deeper darkness at the side of a van. "Come on, girlie," he said. "Don't be scared. You and me can be friends."

"Get away from me! You want m–money, don't you? Sure. Money. Take your hands off me. Let me go. I'll give you money."

His fingers tightened. He dragged her farther into the shadows. "Maybe I take your money. Maybe I take something else, too, huh?"

"No!" Jeanie wrenched her arm, nearly twisting free, stabbing out with her keys, but he caught her with his other hand, spinning her up against a wall. She screamed then, a loud, full-bodied yell that filled the echoing cavern of the garage, reverberating off the concrete surfaces as she fought with the man, slowly losing to his superior strength but not giving even one inch willingly.

She screamed again, the sound cut off by the slap of his filthy hand over her mouth, and then she was falling backward, her keys scraping down the side of his face and neck while darkness came up all around her. Fighting, kicking back with her heels, she struck out, missing the shins she was aiming at and managing to lose one of her shoes. In desperation, she reached up with her left hand, her keys still clutched in her fingers, and raked the sharp point of a key down the man's face. He shouted, jerked his head back, and while he was shifting his grip on her, she sunk her teeth into his hand.

He gave another guttural shout and jerked his hand free, then shoved her forehead hard against the concrete wall. The world spun. Reeling her back toward him, he smacked her with the back of one hand.

Through the red-tinged darkness that swirled around her, she caught sight of an unshaven face with dirty teeth as headlights swept into the cavern of the parking garage and brakes squealed loudly.

There was more shouting. Was she shouting? She didn't know; she knew only that the heavy weight of the mugger was off her. She slumped against the wall, trying to force her wobbly knees to support her. She huddled, hands over her face, listening as the sound of flesh meeting flesh came twice, three times, followed by the dull thud of a body slamming onto the floor.

When hands touched her again, she fought frantically against their hold until the words the man was saying penetrated. "Jeanie, Jeanie, stop fighting me! It's Max!"

"Max? Max! Oh, Max, hold me! Help me!"

He crouched there against the wall, holding her close, rocking her from side to side, one hand stroking her hair back from her face while she clung to him. "Hush, hush. It's all right. He won't hurt you again." He put her shoe on, and said, "Come on, come up here. Let me help you."

Warm hands lifted her. Warm arms enfolded her again. A warm body provided shelter. She shook so, she could barely walk. She burrowed against his broad chest, feeling no surprise at all that Max McKenzie was there, just immense gratitude, safety, and security in his embrace. Just as in every dream she'd had about him, he was a hero.

"Max, he was so dirty! He touched me. He was going to—"

"I know, but stop it. Stop reliving it. He didn't do anything. He won't. Can you move now? I want to get you into the car. I have to call the police."

He put her tenderly on the front seat and let her go only long enough to dash around and get behind the wheel. Then, sliding his arm around her again, he pulled her close, oblivious to the grime on her hands and face and clothes, dirt she was just becoming aware of. He absorbed her shivering with his body as he placed his call, explained the situation curtly, and hung up.

"I should go back over there and make sure he stays put if he comes to," he told her, rubbing the palm of his hand gently over her icy cheek. "Will you be all right now?"

"Don't leave me," she said, her teeth chattering. "Please don't go." Her fingers grabbed onto the lapels of his raincoat. "I know Grandma Margaret gave you to me as a hero for Sharon, but she won't mind if I hold onto you for just a few minutes. I was so scared, Max. So terrified. I thought he was going to rape me!" As she started to tremble uncontrollably, he held her, murmuring soothing phrases without meaning until the shaking finally stopped. Jeanie was too limp to move but continued to lean trustingly against Max's shoulder. He bent to give her a kiss of comfort.

The moment his lips touched hers, though, their kiss escalated into something more.

"Ah, Jeanie, Jeanie," he murmured, lifting his mouth from hers for a second before returning for more of the sweetness he had found there. "I knew it was going to be like this," he told her moments later, his lips skimming over the sensitive skin of her throat. All he could think of was that he had her in his arms at last, and she tasted as wonderful as he had known she would. "I need to touch you, see you, kiss you. For the last week I've been going crazy, wanting to forget I'd ever met you, but still tasting you in my dreams."

Dreams? Dreams? Good heavens! What was she doing? "No, stop!" she cried, pushing him away.

"What?" Lifting his head, he stared down at her, blinking his eyes, slowly coming out of his sensual daze, remembering, realizing where they were and why. "Lord, Jeanie! I'm sorry! Oh, hell, that should never have happened. Forgive me!" He pounded his fist on the steering wheel. "Of all the things to do to you after what you'd been through. Please believe me, I didn't mean for it to happen."

It was difficult to speak, even more difficult to think. She ran a hand through her hair, felt a large lump on her scalp, and winced. It was a bitter reminder of what had gone before and how she had come to be in Max McKenzie's arms.

"It's okay. Okay. I know. It's all right." She was trembling again, but unsure what caused it, the fear or the unexpected passion. "It was as much my fault as it was yours. Maybe it was an excess of adrenaline in both of us." Drawing in a ragged breath, she fumbled in her purse for a tissue and tried in vain to wipe some of the dirt from her face and hands, then attempted, with about as much success, to put her hair back in order. One of her combs was missing. Biting her lip, she looked over at the dim corner where her attacker had dragged her. He still lay there, a mere shape at the edge of the light. Her comb would be there, she knew. And there it would stay. Nothing would make her go back into that corner, not even once the police had come. Where were they? She shuddered convulsively again until Max turned her face away from the sight of her attacker, tucking her head back down against his shoulder. She didn't try to escape his embrace. It felt too good.

"Don't worry," he said. "I'm keeping an eye on him. He hasn't moved. Don't look at him. Don't think about him."

"No," she said, lifting her head again, but not looking into the dark corner by that van. "Thank you. And I'm sorry for falling apart."

"You had every right to fall apart," he said reassuringly, stroking her cheek with the side of a curved finger. That, too, felt good. "Most women I know would have been having screaming hysterics complete with gallons of tears."

"I seldom cry," she said. "And just as seldom let myself get caught in a situation as dangerous as that one was, only the rain made parking on the street anywhere near the restaurant impossible."

"So I discovered too. I'm only glad I had to park up here as well and came along when I did. But when I realized it was you that creep had dragged into the corner, I came close to killing him." Now, he was the one to shudder.

Putting her hand on his shoulder, she said, "No, Max, don't you think about it either. It's all over. You came in time. Remember that."

"I'm trying to. But when I think—" He broke off as a siren echoed in the parking garage. "Here come the police. You stay in the car."

He got out, only to lean back in the window a moment later. "They'll want to talk to you, you know, Jeanie. You'll have to press charges." He sounded almost apologetic.

Jeanie nodded, steeling herself.

"I'm going to drive you home." Max sat behind the wheel of his car, not touching her now but still giving her the feeling of being enfolded by warmth and safety. "I'll get someone to deliver your car, if you'll give me your keys," he went on as he drove down the spiraling ramp toward the street. "You won't want to come back here." She shook her head, and he reached out to take her hand, holding it warmly in his.

"You'll have to tell me your address," he said, nosing the car out onto the street.

It no longer seemed to matter that he was a stranger. Maybe, she thought, because he really wasn't one. He had been there when she needed him. He had held her in his arms. He had comforted her. He had given of himself to her. She told him her address.

"Thank you, Max," she said as he pulled into the visitor parking area at the front of her building. "I'm sorry about dinner." She reached for the door handle. "Good night."

"I'll see you in," he said firmly, getting out of the car. She might have argued, but the clasp of his hand around her elbow made that seem futile, as did the grim set to his jaw. He took her key ring from her, detached what were clearly her car keys, pocketed them, then unlocked the door and stepped back for her to enter. Silently, they climbed five flights of stairs to her floor.

"Would you . . . would you like to come in?" she asked. He smiled and nodded, then followed her inside and closed the door firmly. She turned from him as she unbuttoned her coat and dropped it across the back of a chair in the entry. It was filthy and would have to go to the cleaners in the morning. "I could fix us an omelet or a sandwich or something."

He smiled again, his eyes crinkling up, glittering blue between his thick, dark lashes as he shrugged out of his tan trench coat. "That sounds great. Beating up bullies gives me an appetite. But why don't you point me in the direction of the kitchen, and I'll make the omelets while you get cleaned up. In case you haven't looked, Ms. Leslie, you're a wreck."

She glanced at her hands, saw the smears of her assailant's blood and the grime from the floor of the garage. Her pantyhose were torn, one of her knees was scraped raw, and her velvet skirt was fit only for the garbage. Luckily, her angora sweater was unscathed.

"Thank you. I won't be long," she said, turning and moving quickly across the living room. She was in the shower, standing under the hot spray when she remembered she hadn't pointed him to the kitchen. No matter, though. He would find it. He was a resourceful man—as well as a hero.

"You hurt your hand," she said, glancing up from the light, fluffy omelet he had set before her. She'd smelled the delicious aroma the minute she came out of the bathroom dressed in a warm, loose track suit. She reached across the table and touched the back of his hand near the bruised knuckles. "I'll put some antiseptic on that." She pushed her chair back and stood.

"It'll be okay," he said with a shrug, then spread honey thickly on a slice of toast. His hands moved deftly in spite of their size. A shiver ran down her spine as she remembered the gentle way they had touched her, the tenderness, the caring in his softly stroking palms while he'd comforted her, then the quivering tension in them when she'd responded to his kisses.

"The skin is broken. The cuts might get infected," Jeanie said, ignoring his protest. Seconds later, she returned from the bathroom with the same tube of ointment she had used on her own scraped knee. Gently, she smeared it on Max's hand, then dabbed up the excess with a tissue.

"Thanks," he said. "That feels better. It started to sting when I washed up."

She sat back down and picked up her fork. "You could have said something."

"Uh-uh." He shook his head, grinning. "Heros

don't whine." Then, when she was busy biting into a slice of toast, he said, "Who's Sharon?"

Jeanie swallowed. "My sister. Why? Did she phone while I was in the shower?" There was alarm in her tone. "What did you tell her? Nothing about—"

"No, no! Relax. She didn't phone. I just wondered who she was."

"If she didn't phone, how did you know about her?"

"You mentioned her." He gave her a puzzled look, picked up a piece of bacon, bit it in half, and then said, "You told me I was supposed to be her hero, not yours. Something about your grandmother having said so."

Jeanie stared. "I did? When?"

"After the attack. When we were in the car."

"I don't remember." But suddenly she did and felt a flush rise up her cheeks. What a damn-fool thing to have said!

He shrugged. "No? Never mind, then. I guess it wasn't important."

"No." Jeanie shook her head. "No," she said again. "Not important at all." She forced herself to eat, but even while she devoured her omelet and toast, her stomach quivered and did a few double loops every time she looked up at him.

His shoulders, under the pale blue of his shirt, were even broader than they had appeared under his trench coat and suit jacket. The jacket now hung over the back of his chair, his top two buttons were undone, and his tie pulled loose, showing a tuft of dark hair below the vee between his collarbones.

When they were both finished, he smiled, his gaze on her face, mesmerizing her. He took one of her hands in his, smoothing his thumb across her knuckles. "But my reason for inviting you out to dinner was important, Jeanie."

"Was it?" Her heart did extraordinary things inside her chest. Quickly, she took her hand back from him and avoided that very strange look in his eyes. "So . . . so was my reason for accepting. I was just on the verge of calling you—in fact, in the very act of lifting the phone—when it rang and it was you," she said, talking too fast but unable to slow down. "I got the most interesting request for a temporary job today, and I thought about you immediately." She flicked a quick glance at his face. No need to tell him that she'd done nothing but think of him since last Monday.

"Really?" He shoved his empty plate aside and leaned on the table. "What is it?"

"It's right up your alley, Max. A man wants someone to write—er—something for him."

He tilted his head to one side in that way she was beginning to find characteristic of him—and charming and wonderful. It enhanced his good looks, sent interesting shadows over his craggy face, making him even more mysterious and enigmatic and intriguing. "Something? Can you be more specific than that? How long is that 'something' supposed to be? Is this a serious job offer for a free-lancer, or is it for my article on odd jobs?"

"Well, maybe both." Jeanie considered for a moment, then laughed, that soft yet rich sound that never failed to move Max. He hadn't thought he'd hear it tonight. That she could laugh said a lot about her strength and courage and her ability to recover from trauma. "Yes, I think definitely both," she went on. "As to length, a couple of pages each, minimum. Maybe three or four, and he wants half a dozen of them. Maybe more, he said. It depends on how the first ones are received."

"First what?"

Jeanie looked up at the ceiling, and then flashed him a twinkling smile. "Something I'm sure you're well versed in, Mr. McKenzie," she said innocently. "Just a few little love letters."

Four

Max sat up straight. "Love letters?" He looked utterly disbelieving. "Some guy wants to hire someone else to write love letters? Why doesn't he write them himself?"

"I don't know." She was serious now. "And maybe it's not even a man who wants them."

"Not a man? Why would a woman want to hire someone to write her love letters?"

"I don't know for sure that its a woman. All I have is a letter signed with two initials and a surname, and a box number as an address. If my client's a man, maybe he doesn't feel he knows the right words or isn't romantic enough for the woman he loves, and he really wants to impress her. If it's a woman, maybe she intends to leave them around for a neglectful husband or lover to find, to shake him up or something. Or maybe she just wants something romantic to read in her lonely room at night so she can pretend. Who knows what motivates people? But whoever it is, what he or she is asking is neither illegal nor immoral, so I agreed to try to find someone to take on the task. And," she added, with a persuasive smile, "whoever it is, is willing to pay well." She quoted him the price the client had offered per page, and he whistled loudly.

"Wow! When do I start?"

Jeanie felt a moment's disappointment. She had thought he would refuse at first, that she would have to persuade him. She hadn't thought, by the way he dressed and the kind of car he drove, to say nothing of where he lived, that he was a hungry free-lance writer willing to take on any assignment at all as long as it paid a few dollars.

"Actually," she said, "tonight would be best. The client is in a real hurry. The letter I received asking to have this set up said the first one was needed by the end of the week. Since the letters have to come to me, and I'm to send them on, the sooner the better. Could you have one on my desk by mid-afternoon tomorrow? And after that, he wants one a day until he says to stop. I told him it would be hard to find someone willing to write love letters and—"

"And I was kidding when I said 'when do I start,' " Max said with a grin. "I told you I write nonfiction. I've never been in love, let alone written a love letter, in my life!"

Her breath caught in her throat. "Never?"

"Never. And I don't intend to start now, especially not when those letters are aimed at someone I don't know and will never know. How could I possibly say anything that a strange woman would find interesting or even pertinent? Besides, how would I start each one? 'To Whom It May

Concern, this is to inform you that I love you dearly'?"

Jeanie chuckled. "My client said 'Darling' or 'Sweetheart' would be an appropriate salutation. And he's provided me with a list of clues to give to you—the writer, that is." She retrieved her attaché case, snapped it open, fished out a folded paper, and handed it to him. He took it without opening it, gazing from it to her, bemused.

"For subsequent letters, of course, the writer will need more detailed hints as to subject, and he'll provide that," Jeanie went on. "You know, sort of like, 'Darling, last night was superb. You cook the most elegant stew.' Or maybe, 'Angel, how I enjoyed dancing with you on the beach in the moonlight.' "

He slapped the folded paper on his closed fist. "Right, and, 'You looked so lovely in your silver lamé gown and your gum boots that it stopped my heart dead.' "

"I guess you never have written a love letter," she said. "Or danced on the sand in the moonlight. Gum boots, indeed."

"In this weather, I wouldn't go to the beach without them," he said, collecting their plates and cutlery and carrying them to the sink. Over his shoulder he asked, "Have you?"

She paused, halfway between him and the fridge, butter dish and cream pitcher in her hands. "Have I what, written a love letter?"

He turned, braced his arms back against the counter, and looked at her. "Danced on the beach in the moonlight." For some reason, he knew her answer was important to him. Maybe it all had to do with why he'd asked her out to dinner. They had to get to that, he knew. And soon.

"No." Her voice was as quiet as his. She opened the refrigerator, set the things down, and closed the door.

"Or written a love letter?" He took her arm and steered her through the archway into the living room, as if this were his home not hers, and seated her on the sofa. He sat beside her.

"No."

"Or been in love?"

"I . . . thought I was, once or twice. But I wasn't. Because when it was over, I didn't really care. I guess I've just never been a very romantic person."

"Me either." He leaned closer to her. Her scent was elusive but just as delicious as before, and it was starting to drive him slightly crazy again. "Have you ever received a love letter?"

"Not since Johnny Mason passed me a note in sixth grade and asked if I wanted to 'do it' with him behind the fire station."

His eyes widened. "That was no love letter. That was a mash note."

"If you've never written a love letter, how do you know the difference?"

He grinned. "Maybe because Johnny what's-his-name isn't the only sixth grader to have written a mash note."

"Did you invite someone to go behind the fire station?"

"No. Down to the marina where my dad's boat was moored. And I was in eighth grade by then, I think. Maybe I developed a bit late. Did you?"

"Did I what, develop late or meet Johnny behind the fire station?"

He laughed and leaned back, one arm along the top of the sofa behind her, fingers just touching her shoulder. "Answer either or both, as you like."

"I developed on a fairly normal schedule, and no, I didn't meet him. Not behind the fire station or anywhere else. As a matter of fact, I had to ask my sister what 'do it' meant. When she told me I was heartily offended and quit offering Johnny Mason my peanut butter cookies. I decided I hated him more than I hated peanut butter cookies."

"Good for you. Your sister is older than you are?"

"That's right."

"Are you close?"

"Very close. Our parents were killed in a boating accident when I was twelve and Sharon, eighteen. She raised me after that. She was wonderful to me. Mother, sister, best friend, all rolled into one." She smiled. "And still is."

"Then I'll have to meet her. Soon."

Jeanie stared at him. "What? I mean, why?"

His hand cupped her shoulder as he turned her toward him. "I told you, Jeanie, that I had a very important reason for inviting you to dinner, for wanting to talk to you, to give you a chance to get to know me better. Didn't you wonder even a little bit about that reason?"

"Yes." She swallowed hard. "I guess I did. What was it you had in mind, Max?"

She watched his throat work. He reached up and loosened his gray-and-blue striped tie another couple of inches. "I guess . . . in my own way, I'm asking for the same thing Johnny Mason was. Only I want to do it right. I'd like you to marry me, Jeanie."

For a moment she thought he was joking or

that she hadn't heard right, but his eyes were serious, and she knew there was nothing wrong with her hearing. She had heard his words with perfect clarity. Shock made her inarticulate and held her immobile for an instant, but then she shot to her feet and strode away from him. With the width of the room safely between them, she spun around and stared at him. "Marry you?" She swallowed with effort. "Marry you? For heaven's sake, Max! *Why?*"

He arose but did not approach her. He looked as if he wasn't going to answer, but then he frowned and said slowly, "Why? I . . . I guess I don't know why. To be honest, I didn't expect you to ask that question."

Her heart hammered high in her throat, making speech difficult. "You didn't?" she asked hoarsely. "What did you expect me to say?"

"I realize I'm sounding more and more like an utter idiot, a real jerk, but I guess I just expected you to say yes." His brows drew together. "Or no." She was suddenly certain that *no* was not one of the answers he'd truly expected. Really, the man was out of his mind. And his ego made Everest look little.

"All right," she said. "For the record, no." She returned to the sofa, not to sit but to straighten a cushion. She perched uneasily on the arm, still staring at him, not knowing whether to laugh or get mad. He was the most disconcerting man she had ever met. If she had any sense at all, she'd toss him out this minute. Marry him, indeed! They had met exactly one week ago, had spent one hour in each other's company until this evening. He had sent her flowers, she had responded with a brief, polite thank-you note. It was hardly a basis for making a lifelong commitment. "How could you possibly ask me something like that?" she demanded, her agitation growing. She got to her feet and paced back and forth across the room, never coming near him but never taking her eyes off his face.

"The very first time we spoke, we established that we both hate cages! Believe me, I haven't changed! No matter how liberated a man might persuade himself he is, there are still too many barriers our society permits him to—expects him to—erect around his wife, his . . . his *property*. I've had relationships with men, Max, not many, but a couple, and the minute I told the man I loved him and we began discussing marriage, things began to change. What he planned for the future, his future, became the dominant issue. What he thought was right for us turned out to be what we were going to do, regardless of what I might have wanted or needed. Do you know even one man who's given up a promising career to follow his wife across the continent when a transfer meant a good promotion for her?"

"Might I point out that you are self-employed? The only person who could transfer you across the country would be yourself. And the same applies to me."

"I was just using that as an illustration! As a single woman, I can do whatever I want, whenever I want. I make my own rules, just as you do. But you can do it married *or* single, because you're male. That's the way our society is."

Max should have felt that this was some kind of victory. His proposal had cracked her facade even more than those wild and unexpected moments of passion. Her eyes were so big and so confused that he felt he was staring into a deep sea on a cloudy day. He wanted her desperately, and she had said a very clear and unequivocal no—was still saying it. He hadn't anticipated that. He hadn't foreseen her considering marriage to him as a cage. Something pretty basic inside him told him that marriage to her would be a wonderful thing, not a set of shackles but a bonding, a togetherness he had been missing and wanting for a long time without recognizing that need in himself. The fact that he hadn't realized it until the moment he saw her said something about the rightness of his decision. There had to be some way he could make her understand, some way he could stop her from running from him. He heard a gusty sigh and recognized it as his own. "Marriage wouldn't have to be a cage. We could work around and through our feelings." He decided she might feel easier if she thought he had a few concerns to be resolved as well. "We could try to have one of those marriages that doesn't trap its partners."

She stared at him. "Do I get you right? Are you talking about one of those so-called open marriages? Where you go your way and I go mine, and we get together once or twice a week and compare notes? Or make friends with other, like-minded couples and have 'fun' weekends away together, and it doesn't matter who ends up in whose bed? Tell me, have you heard of a little thing called AIDS?"

The horror and disgust in her tone told him exactly what she thought of those ideas. It echoed his own feelings exactly. "Of course I don't mean that kind of marriage, and not because of AIDS!" he exploded. "To me a marriage is the exclusive territory of two people, and it doesn't include outsiders in any way. If it does, it isn't a marriage, it's an arrangement, and that's not what I want for us."

"Forget it, Max. Forget you ever said it, and I'll do the same. Subject closed."

"The subject is not closed. Can't you even consider it for a few minutes? I mean, you aren't giving me the smallest chance to explain."

"So . . . explain," she invited coolly, even though she knew that nothing he could possibly say would make her consider his proposal—even for a few minutes.

He moved closer until her forbidding attitude stopped him. "From the moment I first saw you, I've wanted you," he said, and then shook his head as if those hadn't been the words he'd meant to say. "I mean, there's something about you that I respond to so powerfully and on a level so deep that I can't ignore it. So, I thought the only way to cure what ails me is to have you and . . . and you don't look like or act like an easy"—he broke off, rubbed his hand over his face, and shook his head—"Oh, hell, I'm doing this so badly, and all I want is to tell you that I feel something for you I've never felt before for any woman in my entire life."

"A physical response?" she asked, aghast at what she was hearing. She stood, fists clenched at her sides, her gaze fixed on his face. His blue eyes were no longer lost in a crinkle of smiles. They were sober, thoughtful, and slightly darkened under the shadow of his drawn brows. His skin was pale.

"It's more than that, I'm telling you! I don't know what it is. I've responded physically to women before, naturally, but not like this. This is big, Jeanie. It's important. So I think we should get married before we do anything about it."

Now she did laugh, but it was a sound with little humor in it. "You're asking me to marry you because you find me physically attractive? That's insane!"

"Is it?" he challenged. "It is, whether we like to admit it or not, the reason most people marry. I just choose to be blunt about it, not to play stupid games and swear undying love for you. To begin with, I don't believe in love. I don't believe it exists. But I do know that what I feel for you is important, that I care about you. If I'd had any doubts as to that, what happened tonight in the garage and my primitive desire to murder that monster who had touched you would have cleared them up. But it's more than caring too. Maybe this intense sexuality is what people mean when they say love. If you've never really been in love, how can you know? You said you only thought you were. What did you feel before that you don't feel now?"

"I don't know. I can't explain it."

"But you aren't denying that you do feel something?"

She was silent for a few moments, then shook her head. "No. I'm not denying that. There is a very definite . . . sexual feeling between us. But that doesn't mean we have to act on it. It doesn't mean that we are going to. We can't. We don't even know each other."

"I know enough about you. I knew enough ten minutes after we met. Maybe even thirty seconds. You stood there, backlit by the sun coming in your office window, your hair escaping into a little halo of curls, your skin all pink and gold, and your eyes filled with panic. You managed to hide the panic quickly, but I knew you so well without even knowing who you were, that I could read it in you. And I know this"—he moved in on her then, lifted one hand and touched the side of her face, drawing his fingertips over her cheekbone—"You have the most beautiful face I've seen, the most touchable skin, and you like me to touch you."

"No . . ." she said on a soft breath, unable to prevent her tongue from flicking over the spot at the corner of her lips where his fingertip had stroked.

"You—" He broke off, swallowing hard as his gaze followed that unconscious motion of her tongue. "Your sex appeal is so strong, I haven't been able to get you out of my mind. For Pete's sake, Jeanie, why do you think we both went to the trouble to, as you put it, establish that we hated cages? It was because we were both aware of the danger we represented to each other's freedom."

She didn't want to answer that. She didn't even want to think about it. She felt the way she guessed a trapped politician must feel. *Deny, deny, deny!* "You're crazy!"

He took her hand and flattened it on his chest. "Feel what you do to my heart rate, Jeanie. You make me crazy, all right! You make me want you like I've never wanted anyone else in my life, and it makes me just as mad as it makes me horny, but I'm not backing off!"

She felt another helpless laugh escape; there was nothing she could do about it, and this time it held genuine amusement—at both of them. The situation was so bizarre that there was nothing to do *but* be amused. "Most men, feeling that way about a woman, would be doing their damnedest to get her into a bed, not a church," she said, shaking her head.

"Yeah. I know." She thought he looked puzzled by his own actions and words, resentful, too, and confused. He frowned. "But maybe this is all because I think it's time I got married. My brother pointed that out shortly before I met you. Minutes before, as a matter of fact. I laughed. I didn't take it seriously at all. Until I saw you. And then I knew that if I was ever going to do it, I was going to do it with you, because you are the right one for me."

She slid her hand from under his, wondering if he could feel the tremor running through her, and stepped clear of him. "Max," she said, "you have to realize that you can't just get married because your brother thinks it's time. Sit down," she said. "Tell me about your brother. And about you. Do you always do what he says you should? Is he older?"

She didn't know why she was doing this. It didn't make any more sense than his impulsive proposal, but she didn't want to send him away without learning more about him and his strange idea. Not that she was considering it for a moment, of course, but for some odd reason, she couldn't just kick him out. Not until she'd heard everything he had to say.

He didn't sit but walked to one of the tall bookcases that flanked the fireplace and ran his fingers along a row of titles. "Rolph's a couple of years younger than I am. I'm thirty-eight, if you're interested," he added almost parenthetically, "and no, I don't usually listen to his suggestions about how to run my life. He was probably joking when he said it anyway. He was making his usual complaint about the way women respond to me."

Jeanie raised her brows and eased herself down onto the cushions of the sofa. "And how is that?" What a question! She knew all too well how she responded to him and was certain that other women did exactly the same. It gave her a bad feeling. She had never liked to be one of a crowd. Not that it mattered. She had no intention of continuing to be one of those women. She could control her responses.

"They—uh—" His cheekbones took on a dark red shade, and his mouth twisted wryly. "Well, let's just say that I've never had trouble getting dates and—Hell! That sounds pretty juvenile, doesn't it? Like I'm a high-school kid bragging. What I mean is women like me. As a general rule. They . . . well, they usually claim to have fallen in love with me. I don't have to do anything to make it happen, and Rolph believes that there's no point in him trying to have a serious relationship with a woman, because the minute he brings her home to meet the family she's going to drop him and make a play for me." He took a large book from the case, opened it at random, and studied the page in front of him. The flush on his face deepened as he assiduously avoided her gaze.

She leaned back and eyed him curiously. He wasn't boasting. She could see that. He was truly abashed at having to tell her about women's reactions to him. "Does that happen?" she asked. "Do your brother's friends drop him and make plays for you?"

He looked up. "Sometimes." He put the book back. "All right. Nearly always." He came and sat in a wing chair opposite her. "Dammit, Jeanie, it's embarrassing!"

"What is? Talking about it or the fact that it happens?"

His mouth twisted sideways again in an expression of distaste. "Both."

"Do you try to stop it from happening?"

He nodded. "Not that it does much good." He looked even more uncomfortable. "Some women just don't want to take no for an answer. They seem to think I can't possibly mean it. That if they feel for me whatever that thing is they insist on calling 'love,' then I have to return the feeling. And I don't. I never have. I never will, because it isn't a real feeling. It's just another name for sex."

"And you think if you were married, it would stop them from coming after you, just like that?"

"Well, yes, of course! I mean, women would see that there'd be no point in chasing after a married man, wouldn't they, and—" He looked miserable as he shook his head. "Well, it wouldn't hurt, anyway. It would give me some kind of an edge. Make a barrier of sorts. I have had a couple of pretty serious, live-in relationships in the last ten years or so. One lasted nearly two years, and during that time, things with other women eased up a bit. So I figured if I were married for real—" He broke off with a helpless shrug.

Jeanie shook her head. "You're pretty naive for a man of thirty-eight, McKenzie. At least about women."

He stared at her. "No I'm not! Lord, if anyone should know about women, it's me! Didn't I just tell you, I can't seem to keep them away? I probably could have married a hundred times, if I'd wanted to. I just never wanted to." He blew out a breath of air, his lips pursed. "Until now. And now I do."

"Right," she said, smiling wryly. "Now you want to give your brother a break, so you're willing to marry someone. That's really weird, Max. Maybe you should write yourself up as one of those people making a strange job offer."

He rose so quickly, she thought he was going to come and drag her off the couch. But he stood where he was, blue eyes snapping with sudden anger and possibly with hurt, although she doubted that. His feelings for her were purely sexual, so how could her refusal cause him emotional pain? His flush faded as he approached her, leaving his face without color. "I'm not willing to marry 'someone'! I want to marry you, specifically you. I thought I had made that clear. That was no job offer, Jeanie. It was a sincere and genuine proposal of marriage, the first and only one I have ever made, and I never expected to have it laughed at."

A spurt of responding anger propelled Jeanie to her feet too. "Forgive me for seeing humor in it, but I'm afraid I can't possibly take it seriously. It might as well have been a job offer the way you made it. What you were doing was propositioning me, Max! Offering a wedding ring in exchange for regular sex and protection against marauding females. Well, thanks, but no thanks! People marry for love or not at all in my book. They marry when their love is so big and so wonderful that they only want each other and they want it forever. *Other* people. As for me, I won't marry, not for love or, as the old saying goes, money. I'll hang onto my freedom with both hands till the day I die! And so should you, since you're a self-confessed cage hater too. Besides, if you were to marry someone and that had the desired effect of getting women out of your hair long enough for your brother to be happily settled, what would happen when a woman came along who wasn't intimidated by your married status? And believe me, women do exist who don't care if a man's married or not! If you wanted her, you'd be free to go after her, wouldn't you? There's be none of that neat little emotion known as love that sometimes holds people back from hurting others."

His expression gentled. "Is that why you're refusing me, Jeanie? Because you're afraid I'd hurt you?"

She sighed in exasperation. "No, Max. I'm refusing because we don't love each other. We don't even know each other!"

He stepped so close, she could smell the subtle scent of his cologne. She wished she didn't have to breathe, but more than just an autonomic reflex dictated that she draw in deep drafts of it. "We could get to know each other. If love makes self-respecting people act the way I've seen some women—and guys—act, then I'm glad I can't feel it. I'd hate to look like a fool. But that doesn't mean I can't feel, Jeanie."

His hands were warm on her arms. She knew she could pull away from him, that he wouldn't stop her, but he was like a magnet drawing her closer. Her breasts brushed the front of his shirt, her nipples peaking instantly, pushing out the fabric of her sweatshirt. She saw a flicker in his eyes, knew he felt their hardness against his chest, and knew he was pleased by it.

"Max . . ." Her voice cracked. Her mouth was dry. She licked her lips. "Max, I . . ."

"Yes, you do," he murmured, and she knew now that he could read her mind. "You want this as much as I do, Jeanie." One of his hands slid up over her shoulder, then lifted to cup her chin, his thumb brushing over her full lower lip. "But I won't do it until you say I can."

She lifted a hand to place it against his arm, meaning to shove him away, but her fingers discovered the solidity of his biceps, curled around, and slid higher. Dimly, she heard the faint tinkle of golden bangles and her own voice saying, "Yes . . ." on a soft, helpless sigh.

"Yes . . . you'll marry me?"

Startled, she drew back and saw his blue eyes dancing with light. A laugh escaped her, surprising her. "No! Of course not. But you could . . . kiss me."

"Ahh . . . yes," he murmured, drawing her into a full embrace. "That will do for now."

It was a magic kiss, slow and sweet and undemanding, letting trust build along with need, so that when his tongue slipped through the narrow opening between her lips, she was ready to welcome it and greet it with her own. A heavy fluttering began deep in Jeanie's body, warming her until she felt as if she glowed all over. One of Max's hands splayed across the small of her back, moving slightly up and down, his fingers curved to massage her flesh. The other hand tugged at her hair tie, slid it free, and then plowed through the thick mass of curls, spreading them over her shoulders, around her face. His mouth left hers as he buried his face in her thick hair, breathing in its scent, murmuring his appreciation. His lips caressed her cheeks, her closed eyes, her earlobe. His teeth nibbled gently beside her earring. "Jeanie . . ." he said softly, and let her go, steadying her for a moment before stepping back.

"Ahh . . . Jeanie, you are so sweet. So wonderful to hold, so perfect to kiss. I have to leave now. I have to say good night while I still can," he said, cupping her flushed face between his hands. Dropping a kiss on her nose, he added, "I'll see you tomorrow."

"No." She moved away from him, shaking her head, her arms wrapped tightly around herself.

He picked up his jacket, shrugged into it, then draped his raincoat over his arm. "No? Why not?" His expression told her clearly that he didn't believe her, that he had no intention of taking no for an answer.

"Because I don't think we should see each other again."

He smiled. "How can we get to know each other properly if we don't?"

"We aren't going to get to know each other properly." She paused, seeing the light of laughter rise in his eyes once more, knowing what he was about to say. She said it first. "Or improperly, for that matter." Dammit, why did he have to be so totally charming? She felt sorry for his brother. Maybe she *should* take him out of circulation to give poor Rolph a chance and—Hey! She had to get a grip on those crazy thoughts!

"Nothing is improper between two consenting adults," he said, looking at her.

"What you're thinking is," she retorted.

His chuckle was warm, as warm as his breath when he bent forward and nuzzled her neck for an instant. "How can you be so sure what I'm thinking? Because you're thinking the same things?"

He was probably right, but she didn't have to admit it.

"Good night," she said. "Thank you again for rescuing me. It was very nice of you to drive me home, but that doesn't mean we need to see each other again."

"Jeanie, I like you. In addition to whatever else I might feel, I really do like you. Couldn't we at least be friends?"

"No," she said crossly. "I mean, how in the world could I possibly be friends with you as long as that crazy proposal of marriage is hanging over my head?"

"That's not very flattering. You make my proposal sound like a poised guillotine."

"It makes me feel as if there's one up there. Just the idea of putting myself at a man's mercy makes me shudder."

He stepped back from her, his head tilted to one side, a questioning look on his face. "At a man's mercy? You think we're living in the fifteenth century or something? Those are pretty strong words."

She blew out an explosive breath. "I feel strongly about it. I saw what happened to my sister after she got married, how little actual say she had in what happened to her, how loving, marrying, took all her personal control away, turned her into a reflection of what her husband, Ellis, wanted her to be. It was terrible!"

"Tell me about it," he invited gently.

She shook her head. "Maybe. Someday."

He smiled, and her stomach flipped over. "Someday? Does that mean you've changed your mind, and we'll be seeing each other again? Getting to know each other is going to be so exciting! I'm glad you've changed your mind."

She had to laugh. It was annoying, but this man had the capacity to make her see the humor in situations. "No, it doesn't mean that at all, and I have not changed my mind. It was just a figure of speech, sort of a promise to get rid of a guy."

"It's not going to be that easy for you to get rid of me, you know."

She sighed. "I'm beginning to realize that. But maybe you should know at the outset that I don't find men particularly trustworthy. I know I'd find it impossible to trust enough ever to enter into anything but the most casual of relationships. No cages, Max. Ever."

Max nodded, moving close to her. "I understand, Jeanie."

"Do you?" She forced herself not to back up.

"Yes. You don't believe that I could just accept friendship with you."

Her smile became more genuine. "I think you've made it pretty clear you'd want more than that, Max."

"Ahh . . . that ax hanging over your head?"

"Something like that."

"Okay, I hereby withdraw my proposal of marriage. I want your friendship."

"Uh-uh!" She had to laugh at him again. "If we were to be friends, then we'd have to see each other again, right?"

"Of course we'd have to see each other. Friends do. And anyway, didn't you say you wanted the first love letter on your desk by tomorrow?" He drew a finger from her temple to her chin as if he couldn't leave without touching her just one more time.

She forced herself to ignore the sensations his brief touch had left curling within her body, forced herself to put on her most professional face, her most formal tone. She could have had her sturdy oak desk between them, instead of a mere three inches of heated air, air that shimmered with undeniable desire. "Oh? You're taking the job, then, Mr. McKenzie?"

Seeing his smile, she knew he wasn't fooled in the least. "That's right, Ms. Leslie. I'm accepting the position."

"Even though you don't write fiction?"

"I'll think of you when I'm writing. That way, it won't be fiction."

"Excuse me, but those are supposed to be love letters, remember. Not mash notes."

He looked blank for a moment. "There's a difference?" And then, with another grin, and a tiny, almost undetectable touch of his index finger against her lower lip, he turned and let himself out. It wasn't until then that she realized he'd left the sheet of instructions for the first love letter lying on the end table. She sighed. Okay, so he hadn't been serious about taking the job.

She shouldn't be surprised, she supposed. He was, after all, a man. Oh, yes! He was a man.

Five

Jeanie stood staring at the door for several minutes, then sank back down onto the couch, lifting her hands to tame the wild hair he had set free. Again, she heard the faint tinkle of gold bangles and looked sideways at her arm. It was bare but for the shoved-up sleeve of her sweatshirt. She had removed the bracelets earlier when she changed, yet she distinctly recalled hearing them jangle at the moment she'd surrendered to Max's kiss.

"All right, Grandma Margaret," she said. "What in the heck are you up to? Just go away. Leave me alone. Keep out of my love life!" With that, she went to bed.

Love life? The words snapped back into her mind as she was about to slide into sleep and shocked her wide awake. Now, wait a minute! She didn't have a love life, dammit! She didn't know who she was telling, her long-departed ancestoress or herself, but it didn't matter. Thinking about it kept her from having nightmares about awful men in dark parking garages—and dreams about blue-eyed heros with magic kisses. She awoke feeling more energetic than she had in many months, and much more eager to face the day.

Her car was parked in the correct slot the next morning, and when she unlocked it with her spare key, she found her missing antique comb tucked into a small envelope on the passenger seat along with the other keys. She stroked the comb, unutterably glad to have it back, and so grateful to Max McKenzie that she could have wept—only weeping was not her thing. There was also a bright red full-blown rose lying across the dash. She picked it up, sniffed its heady scent, and laid it carefully on the seat beside her before starting the engine. As little as she knew him, she recognized that the rose was as characteristic of Max McKenzie as his charm. No tight little bud that she would have to wait to see in its full glory from him. He was showing her how it could be, right now, no waiting, no tiptoeing around each other. He'd said that he didn't play games. He wanted her, wanted what they could create, wild and full and magnificent in its richness.

She swallowed a thick lump that suddenly filled her throat, a lump that tasted strangely of fear. Because, when it came right down to it, she had to admit that she was probably just as eager as he that things between them progress far more rapidly than her mind told her was wise. In fact, if she were to listen only to her mind, she'd drive the car aboard the next ferry to the mainland and head out east, driving as far and as fast as she could. She wondered briefly what Newfoundland was like in October.

The trouble was, she didn't have only a wise mind to contend with; she had an aching body with a memory all its own and a growing need for something she hated to put a name to. But as she drove her usual route between home and work, she realized that she had never felt so alive; the world had never looked so bright. The air was completely clear, there was no morning haze that so often masked the gulf and blurred the view of the off-shore islands. Six miles away across Haro Strait, San Juan stood glowing with maples turned out in autumn gold and dogwoods in burgundy red, interspersed throughout the rich shades of the evergreens on its steep flanks. Nope. Newfoundland could have nothing to compare to this other island a whole continent away. She'd stay, regardless of the consequences.

She should have been happy to feel so good, considering the close call she'd had the previous night. She was happy, of course. She was glad that the horror had been wiped away so effectively by subsequent events. She just wished those subsequent events wouldn't keep filling her mind, flooding her senses with delicious memories she'd be better off without. She shivered, remembering warm kisses, thrilling touches, soft murmurs, gasped words of mutual delight. She smiled, recalling another smile that she was totally incapable of resisting.

"Max McKenzie," she said aloud, "why don't you just take your charm and your good looks and your crazy proposal of marriage, your red rose and . . . and . . . write bogus love letters instead?"

He did.

The first one was on her desk, not by the middle of the afternoon, but by the middle of the morning, and because he had forgotten or perhaps simply not bothered to take the initial list of instructions her client had provided, she knew the letter on her desk would be all wrong even without reading it. How could she send it to the client? It couldn't possibly contain any of the right material.

She knew she should have consigned it to the shredder the moment she realized what it was. She hadn't thought of reading the letters her client had requested. All she'd been contracted to do was find the writer, accept his work, and forward it to the box number the client had given, thereby providing an added measure of anonymity for him. Or her.

But Max had sent it sealed inside a courier's envelope, with PERSONAL written big and bold across the front. Even Cindy had noticed and not opened it. Jeanie's eyes widened and her heart began to pound as she scanned the letter. Before she had read more than four or five of the neatly typed, double-spaced lines, she was hooked and hoped that the client wasn't a woman trying to make a man jealous, because if that were the case, then the letter from Max was certain to do the job. She'd hate to be an inadvertent accessory to murder.

It read,

Sweetheart,

When I got home last night, I stripped off my clothes and headed toward the shower, but halfway there I realized that if I bathed, I'd be washing away every vestige of your scent that remained on my skin. I put my shirt back on, because your cheek had rested against it, your hair had brushed over its fabric, your body had been pressed to it. It smelled of you. When I climbed into bed, I still wore it, pretending that your arms, not just scented cotton, were wrapped around me, that you clung to me as tightly as did that shirt. Would that it had been more than mere fantasy! I spent most of the night thinking about you, and when I fell asleep in the early hours, my dreams were filled with you. I heard your husky laugh. I saw your smoky eyes. I felt your warm, soft lips under mine again and again, parted and sweet, accepting all I cared to give, and I cared to give everything. And in my dreams you wanted all I could give and gave your all in return. Your tangled, curly hair wrapped itself around my hands and wrists, brushed my chest, tantalized my belly. I ached for you, and when I awoke, my first thoughts were of you.

I want never to leave you at night again. I want to find you in my arms every morning. To have your face beside mine on my pillow would be the nearest thing to heaven I could imagine. Think about it, my sweet. Think about opening your sleepy eyes and seeing me. Think about my slowly sliding the covers back inch by inch, kissing your warm skin, discovering your shape, your hard nipples. Would they be hard with wanting me that quickly, or would I need to tease them into awareness? I'd do it anyway for our mutual pleasure, but I think they'd be ready, ripe, full, because I know how aroused I am just writing these words. What does reading them do to you?

"My God! It's a mash note," Jeanie whispered to herself, turning over the page and staring at its blank back. It didn't help. The words were burned into her brain. She gulped, bit her lip, and wondered if he really had to ask what reading them did to her. What they did was extraordinary, unbelievable! They were only words typed on paper, for heaven's sake! Yet, she was responding to them exactly as if he were right there, touching her, breathing on her skin, whispering them in her ear. Almost against her will, she flipped the page back over and read on.

When I see you again, I'll ask you that question. You won't be able to evade me or equivocate. I'll look into your gray eyes and know the truth.

"Oh, heaven help me! He would too!" she muttered. "Lord, what am I going to do?"

I want to see you right this minute. I want to hold you, touch you, smell your scent. When are you going to spend the whole night with me, my sweet? When are you going to release me from the torture of wanting to have you with me always, ease the agony of having to wait?

It's the waiting that's intolerable. Don't make me wait any longer. Call me, dear heart. Call me and tell me our time is now.

I won't sign my name because you know who I am. Simply, the man who wants you more than he's ever wanted anyone else in his life.

When she was able to move, Jeanie reached for the phone. When she was sure she'd be able to speak instead of just breathe heavily, she dialed and drew in several steadying breaths, listening to the ringing at the other end. When a female voice responded with the information that she had reached Max's office, she was able to say, "I'd like to speak to Mr. McKenzie, please," with a cool briskness in which she took great pride. "J. Leslie Career Consultants calling."

"I'm sorry, Mr. McKenzie is working just now, and I can't interrupt him until twelve forty-five, unless the house is on fire, and not even then unless it's burning in this wing. I'm Freda Coin, his personal assistant. Maybe I can help you?"

The woman sounded as if she were accustomed to deflecting interruptions. She also sounded as if she were always successful, and as if perhaps her middle name were Legree. Jeanie, however, had never been put off by tough people. She hadn't become the president of her own company two years ago at the age of twenty-nine by allowing others to keep her from what she meant to accomplish.

"Mr. McKenzie is under contract to do some

work for one of my clients. I really must speak with him at once," she said clearly in her politest yet most determined tone. "It is very important, and I know he'll want to talk with me."

"And I'm certain he will, my dear, just as soon as he is able. But as I told you, Mr. McKenzie is working. As you likely know, that means writing. When he is at his word processor, he permits no one and nothing to interrupt him. It would be more than my life was worth to knock on his door before his lunch arrives. Even then, I knock, open it, and shove his tray in with a long pole. Mr. McKenzie is not an easy man to disturb."

Jeanie thought briefly of disputing that statement, but the kind of "disturbing" she'd be speaking of was not what his assistant meant. Freda Coin sounded somewhat older than the women who were likely to be chasing Max McKenzie, but perhaps age was no barrier to the man's fatal charm. Freda continued. "I'd be happy to take your name and number and have him call you when he's able."

Not accustomed to such obdurate refusals, Jeanie's tolerance level began to slip. "That," she said, "might make you happy. It might even make Max happy. It would not, however, make me happy, Ms. Coin. I need to speak to him, and it's imperative that I do it now. He has submitted an extremely unsatisfactory piece of work and it needs immediate attention."

"And I'm quite positive he will be glad to give it that attention when he is finished what he is doing. Believe me, I'll pass on your message along with all the others just as soon as I am able. What did you say your name was?"

"I didn't. I am Jeanie Leslie of J. Leslie Career

Consultants. I suggest, madam, that you tell him who is on the line. He will take my call, I assure you."

"No, he won't. At least not while he's writing. I'm truly sorry, but I won't interrupt him," said the firm, unflappable voice of Freda Legree Coin.

Jeanie decided on a swift change of tactics, preceded by a soft, understanding laugh. "Of course," she said. "We all know what grouches men can be when they're working. But I assure you, Freda, he'll want to hear from me. So please, as one woman to another, won't you make an exception to your excellent, and I'm certain necessary, rule, and at least tell him I'm calling? Let him make the decision."

Freda's laugh was not soft nor was it gentle. It was filled with genuine amusement and a little malice. "Sweetie," she said, "Max pays me well to make those decisions for him. I fend off at least a dozen calls like yours every day, and every one of you assures me that Max would really want me to make an exception in her case. Now why should I think you're any different?"

"Because," said Jeanie, "I am. Last night, Max asked me to marry him."

There was a very long silence at the other end and then another laugh, this one filled with an odd combination of admiration and sympathy. "Now, that," said Freda, "takes the year's—no, maybe even the decade's—prize for inventiveness. Bye-bye, sweetie pie. I'll tell him you called."

"Wait!"

There was an impatient sigh, then a curt "Yes?"

"Tell me," said Jeanie. "Which wing of the house am I going to have to set on fire?"

"The west one," said Freda. "But only if you can get past the pit bulls." Then, she hung up.

Jeanie did the same and found to her amazement that she was laughing again. Freda Coin would probably be as much fun to know as Max McKenzie.

The light on her phone flashed twenty minutes later, and she picked it up to hear Cindy say, "Mr. McKenzie for you on line three."

Jeanie grinned. "Tell him I'm in conference and can't be disturbed unless the building's on fire, and then only if the fire's on the fourth floor."

"But what if it's on the second or third floor, Ms. Leslie? Or even the first? Wouldn't you want to get out? Uh . . . would it be okay if I got out? I mean, after I told you, of course?"

"Sure, Cindy. If the building ever catches fire, you let me know and then get on out, no matter what floor it's on. But in the meantime, simply tell Mr. McKenzie what I said and that I have found his work unsatisfactory. I will be sending him further instructions by messenger. Okay?"

"You don't want to talk to him?"

"I don't want to talk to him."

Cindy sighed dramatically. Clearly, she thought Jeanie was several flakes short of a snowball. *Any* woman who passed up an opportunity to talk to Max McKenzie had to be short something.

Jeanie hung up and went back to the résumé she was working on. It wasn't easy to make a man who had been fired from three different executive positions in five years look like a good prospect, but she was obligated to try.

She had just unearthed from her notes the fact that he had once brought a company back from near bankruptcy by an inventive method of marketing, when a piercing scream split the air and Cindy's panicked voice cried, "Help! He's lighting a fire in the wastebasket! Stop! No! Ms. Leslie! Quick! What should I do?"

Jeanie flew out of her chair at the word fire, barked her shin on the leg of her desk, and bashed her hip into the arm of her visitor's chair trying to get out of the room. By the time she'd heard the word wastebasket, she'd flung open her office door and come to a halt to see a grinning Max McKenzie aiming a small, red fire extinguisher into the wastebasket from which a tiny wisp of smoke emerged. A bug-eyed Cindy was backed up against the filing cabinets, wringing her hands, and several heads poked around the door, all wearing variously stunned or interested expressions on their faces.

"What," asked Max much too loudly, "was wrong with that love letter I sent you, Jeanie Leslie? I think for a first attempt it was damned good. Didn't you like that part about me wearing my shirt to bed because it smelled like you? And how about the part where I said I never wanted to wake up again without seeing your face on the pillow beside mine, and the part about how I'd slowly move the covers down until I could see your—"

He broke off as she grabbed a fistful of his thick, curly dark hair and literally dragged him, extinguisher and all, into her office, kicking the door shut behind her.

"I am going to trade that girl in on a pit bull and turn it loose on you! You are a menace, Max McKenzie! A—"

He reached up with his free hand and untangled her fingers from his hair, then kissed her palm before she thought to snatch her hand away. But his reaction had the effect of stopping her flow of words to say nothing of her flow of breath.

"As you might have guessed," he said with a grin, "I heard about your conversation with Freda. She was highly amused and wants to meet you. Especially because you told her you intend to marry me."

Jeanie gasped. "I did nothing of the sort! I merely told her that you'd proposed."

"To Freda, it would be inconceivable for you to have refused. She's probably out right now looking for a new hat."

"Hat?"

"To wear to our wedding."

"She is not! She didn't even believe me."

"She did once I told her that I had asked you. By the way, when is it going to be?"

"It isn't going to be, you idiot! Remember, you withdrew your proposal."

"Why, so I did. How forgetful of me. I must remember to tell Freda that when I get home. Maybe she can take the hat back."

"Maybe she can save it to wear to your funeral." Jeanie whirled around, grabbed the two pages of his letter that she'd hidden under her blotter, and waved them in his face.

"What kind of garbage is this? I thought you took that job offer seriously, Max. I can't send this to my client! For one thing, a real love letter would never be typewritten! And for another, what if the person it's meant for doesn't have curly hair or gray eyes, as you specifically mentioned? What if the real recipient *does* actually wake up in the morning with her head on the same pillow as the writer, and he does . . ." She broke off, swallowing hard, but he didn't hesitate to fill in the silence.

"And he does pull down the covers, inch by inch—"

"Dammit, stop that! This is a business office not a boudoir!" She was glad that she was wearing a suit with a boxy bouclé jacket. Quickly, she sat behind her desk and folded her arms on top of her blotter. "Sit down. We have to discuss this like professionals, if you mean to go on with the job. Otherwise, I'll have to find someone else."

To her surprise, he sat down, bouncing the little red extinguisher on his knees as if it were a baby. "All right, so make any changes you feel are appropriate. Just get your secretary, receptionist, whatever she is, to type it up and send it to your client."

Jeanie shuddered at the thought of asking Cindy to type copies of that letter. She shuddered at the thought of trying to type them herself. She valued her office equipment far too highly to want to watch it catch fire. His word processor would have to have a cast-iron casing.

She looked at him with studied patience. "These letters cannot be typewritten. That's why the client insisted I hire a male writer for the job, so that they would be in a distinctly masculine hand."

Max's dark brows rose. "Couldn't he write them himself? I mean, copy out something someone else typed?"

"Max, remember we don't know if the client is male or female, and really, I don't ask questions like that. When someone wants me to find an employee, unless he's looking for a hired gun, I find what he wants. If I haven't done so in this case, tell me now and I'll start advertising, which is what I should have done in the first place."

"He—you keep saying he. Jeanie, what if the other possibility is the right one and the client is a woman? And *she* wants them in *my* handwriting? I could be setting myself up for a breach of promise suit or something."

"Don't be ridiculous." She laughed. "Suits like that went out with spats."

He grinned. "Hadn't you noticed? Spats are back in. You and I have them all the time. If I write these letters for you, you're going to have to protect me by accepting my proposal of marriage."

"As I pointed out before, you withdrew your proposal."

His eyes danced. "Can't I reinstate it?"

Jeanie had to laugh again. Dammit, the man made her feel so giddy, she couldn't even conduct a proper job interview! "No, you cannot! Now, are you taking this job, Mr. McKenzie? Are you in or are you out? Are you going to cooperate, or are you not?"

"You don't need to trade Cindy in on a pit bull." He glared at her for a moment. "You seem to do all right yourself. If Freda ever quits, maybe I'll hire you."

"Not likely. I've moved beyond that stage of my career, but perhaps you could hire someone I've trained," she said sweetly. "By the time I've finished with them, they all know how to bite, and the bitee rarely knows that he's been wounded until he finds himself bleeding. And usually, by then, my trainee has what she wants. And you haven't answered my question."

"All right," he said with a brief nod. "Give me

the list of requirements and I'll do my best. I'll have a love letter to suit your client's needs on your desk before five this evening."

"Thank you."

"On one condition," he said smoothly.

Jeanie sighed. "What is that?"

"That you have lunch with me. Because Freda told me you called, and you refused my return call, I missed my lunch."

"You mean the one she pokes into your room at twelve forty-five with a long pole?"

He blinked. "She said that? The old—just for that, I'm going to take away her laser printer."

Jeanie gulped, wondering if Freda had been the one to run off that letter on her laser printer, but all she said was, "A crueler punishment I can't imagine."

He stood. "Are you ready?"

She remained seated. "For what?"

"Lunch."

"No, Max. Our relationship is purely business."

"Right," he said, then set the extinguisher on her desk and turned, closing the door quietly behind him as he left. Jeanie sighed, hid the pages of his letter in the bottom of a drawer, and went back to the résumé she'd been struggling with when he'd set Cindy's wastebasket on fire.

She had finished the résumé, taken a package of cheese and crackers from a shelf in the credenza, poured herself a cup of coffee, and was spreading crumbs across her desk when the letter somehow materialized on her blotter again. She reread it, wondering if the extinguisher was fully expended just in case it was needed, sighed again, and started at the top once more. There was something about that letter that was too compelling for her to shove it through the shredder; it brought back too many of the previous night's sensations. Was that what a love letter was supposed to do? If it was, then Max McKenzie had missed his calling. He should have been a gigolo!

When the door of her office opened, she jumped and folded her arms across the incendiary pages, terrified of Cindy's reaction should she see them. It was bad enough that she—along with several others from adjacent offices—had heard Max start quoting from the damned thing. The gossips must be having a ball. "What—" *What is it?* she had started to say to her receptionist, but her word choked off as Max, laden with Chinese food bags, came in and dumped the packages on her desk.

"Lunch," he said, and handed her another full-blown rose, this time a yellow one. "Since you didn't comment on the red one, I thought maybe you hadn't liked it."

Slowly, she stood. "I liked it," she said through an oddly tight throat. "And I like this one too. Thank you, Max. And especially, thank you for returning my comb. It is something I value highly. It belonged to my dad's great-grandmother. She was a Gypsy."

He came around to her side of the desk, sat down in her chair, and pulled her onto his lap, leaning around her shoulder to look at the papers on her desk.

"And you liked that, too, didn't you?" he asked with what barely missed being a smug grin.

"Damn you!" she said. "Oh, damn you, Max McKenzie!" But then she kissed him with all the scary, wonderful feelings that were growing inside her like the full-blown rose that was being crushed between their tightly melded bodies.

He broke the kiss long enough to say, "Yeah, and damn you, too, Jeanie-the-Gypsy Leslie."

Six

"Max, what are we doing?" she said moments later, when she was able to speak. He cradled her head in his hands and smiled at her. "Getting in the mood."

"I was beginning to get the impression that you were always in the mood." And, that when he was around, so was she, she added silently. She pushed his arms away from her and got unsteadily off his lap. "Out," she said. "Out of my chair." He stood, and she sat down, immediately aware of the heat his body had left behind. "I should also say 'out of my office,' but I'm starving and that food smells wonderful."

Taking the visitor's chair, he set it close to hers and opened the first of the bags on her desk, lifting out two round, foil-topped dishes. "Where you're concerned, I *am* always in the mood," he said, lifting the lid off the first dish. The scent wafting up around her made Jeanie swiftly forget her cheese and crackers, and she eagerly delved into another bag.

They ate with their fingers and plastic forks, munching on egg rolls, dipping into chow mein, deep-fried prawns, and sweet-and-sour boneless pork, sharing the dishes as if they'd been picnicking together all their lives. While they ate, they talked and laughed and enjoyed each other, arguing sometimes, agreeing on most subjects, though, and discovering a mutual passion for Roy Etzel.

"Nobody, but nobody can play a trumpet the way he does. When he plays *Il Silenzio* I put my life on hold until the last notes fade away," Jeanie said.

"I know. He's incredible." He licked his fingers and began stuffing plum and soy sauce packages into one of the empty bags, then gave her a sheepish grin and a sideways glance. "I play the trumpet a little myself, you know. Sometimes I dream that if I keep on, I'll find the magic he has. You know, the way he hits every note with absolute clarity? I'll never make it, of course, but everyone's entitled to a dream, no matter how crazy or futile it might be."

She was oddly touched that he'd revealed such an intimate facet of his personality. She laid her hand over his briefly before moving away; being close to the man was too tempting. Without any encouragement at all, she could find herself back in his arms. "Maybe, in time, you will. If you have the heart for it and the talent, then surely all it takes is practice."

"I have the heart, but I'm afraid I lack the talent. Besides, I only practice when there's no one around for miles and miles."

Jeanie spoke over her shoulder from where she

was dampening a paper towel in her private bathroom. "Where do you find that kind of privacy?"

As she returned, he took the towel from her and began wiping the sticky spills off her desk. "About halfway up the Malahat, accessible only by air or down a long and winding private road fit only for mountain goats and four-by-fours, I've got a tiny cabin. It's one room and a lean-to, perched on a bluff high over a little lake. There's never anyone else around, and that's where I play my trumpet." He stopped what he was doing and looked out into space, a half-smile on his lips, his eyes seeing things only he could see, his ears attuned to something in his memory. "It sings for me there," he added softly, "echoing out over the lake and bouncing back from the hills. Up there, it's the only entertainment I need, the only companionship. There, I can almost believe I'm good." He shrugged and his mouth twisted. "Sort of like singing in the shower, I guess."

She smiled gently. "Maybe you are good, Mac. You must have had lessons. What did your teachers say?"

"No lessons," he said. "I can't even read music. An old friend of my dad's gave me his trumpet to play with one day when I was a kid. We were out on the boat. He showed me how to get sounds out of it, and I seemed to catch on right away. He was so amazed, he bought me one of my own and wanted me to take lessons. He wanted to *give* me lessons. I was eleven or so and thought music lessons were for sissies. Besides, it turned out I really didn't need them in order to get music out of the horn. I just sort of play and the right notes . . . happen . . . at the right time and place. If I hear a tune a couple of times, I can usually come up with a pretty close approximation of what the composer had in mind."

She stared at him. "I'd like to hear you someday."

"Then you'd have to come up to my cabin and visit me. I've never entertained anyone there, but I think I could stand sharing it with you." The way he said it and the way he looked at her as he spoke made her quiver deep inside. If she went to his cabin, it wouldn't be just to hear him play the trumpet, and they were both very much aware of that.

She had to get her mind off the ramifications of her and Max alone in a remote cabin with only each other—and a trumpet—for entertainment. She didn't think the trumpet would get much use.

"Thanks," she said. "But I lack the necessary ingredients for a trip to your cabin. I don't have a four-by-four. Nor do I have wings."

He grinned. "Neither do I, but I do have a helicopter and a small landing pad. Would that do? I could take you and my trumpet and see what kind of music the three of us could make together."

"That," she said, "sounds decidedly kinky, Mr. McKenzie."

His grin widened and his eyes danced. "Yeah. I thought so too."

"You'd fascinate my sister," she told him.

He raised his brows. "Your sister likes kinky trumpeters?"

"I doubt it, but it would likely break her heart to know there's a natural like you running around loose without any training at all. She's a musician, a fine harpist, trained at the Royal Conservatory. A composer, too, but she doesn't do much of that anymore. She rarely even plays her harp." Jeanie sighed. She didn't like to talk about Sharon's having turned her back on her music, the stuff of her very existence. She hated even to think of it. Especially now, because it had been her desperate hope that a different interest in life—namely a man—might be the catalyst needed to turn Sharon around. That hope was what had introduced her to Max McKenzie.

He tilted her face up with one finger. "You look sad. Tell me."

She shook her head. "Nothing to tell. Just a passing thought. More a memory than anything. An unwelcome one." She glanced at her watch. "I have to get back to work, Max, and I'm sure you do too. Or Freda Legree will be hot on your tail."

"I'm going to tell her you called her that."

"Go ahead. I don't expect I'll ever meet her."

"Yes, you will. And by the way, she has instructions that you can interrupt my writing any time of the day or night. Call, and you'll be put right through, no arguments, no burning down the west wing, no pit bulls to fight off." Cradling her face between her hands, he kissed her hard and deeply, sliding his hands into her hair, loosening it from its confining clips. When she was limp and compliant against him, he whispered against her lips, "You taste delicious."

"So do you." She couldn't stop herself from taking another taste. "Soy sauce, sesame seeds, and Max."

"Oh, no," he murmured huskily moments later, "that's soy sauce, sesame seeds, and Jeanie." Then, as if he'd made a very firm decision, he added, "You will meet Freda, you know. And you'll meet my brother, as well as my mother and father. Come home with me for dinner tonight, Jeanie." It sounded more as if he were saying *Come home with me to bed tonight, Jeanie,* and she didn't know which she was refusing when she shook her head.

"Too soon?" he asked, his head tilted to one side.

"It's not that. It's just that there's no point."

"Ah, Jeanie, don't keep kidding yourself. We belong together. And one way or another, we are going to be together."

She shivered, knowing he was right. It was inevitable. She, who resisted casual affairs, seemed about to embark on one, although just how casual it would turn out to be was another question. The only thing she knew for sure was that no relationship she had was going to be of a legal nature. That way, if she needed out, she could just walk away. There'd be no male-dominated court system to take away everything she had ever worked for and award it to a man, simply because he had the money to hire the better lawyer.

She drew in a deep, unsteady breath. "You can come to my place tonight for dinner if you like." Even as she said it, she wondered if dinner were all she meant to offer him.

His smile had the power of a dozen suns. "What time?"

"Eight?"

"I'll be there."

"Okay. And in the meantime, will you redo the first letter for me? I'd really like to get it away to my client tomorrow."

"Sure," he said easily. "I'll bring it with me tonight, and you can okay it." After another quick kiss, he turned and strode from her office, leaving the door ajar. Through the crack she heard Cindy giggle and wondered what he had said to the girl. No doubt it was something charming that would have her receptionist dreaming dreams of a black-haired hero with blue, blue eyes.

She shut the door. "Sorry, Cindy," she said. "He's too old for you."

And too dangerous for you, she told herself. But only a very tiny, insignificant part of her even bothered to listen.

"I forgot to ask," Max said, entering her apartment with an armful of white roses mixed with purple flags and frothy greenery. "Can you cook?"

She shrugged. "About as well as you write mash notes."

He grinned. "Wow! I'm impressed! What are we having, stuffed squab? Lobster thermidor? Pheasant under glass?"

"Such an ego! I refuse to feed it. Instead, I'll feed you beef Stroganoff, hot buttered noodles, and *Salade Jeanie.*" With a smile, she took the flowers and led the way into the kitchen where she placed the bouquet on the table as she rummaged under the sink for a large enough vase.

"Artistic, too, I see." Max watched closely as she twitched one of the irises into a slightly different position and added another tuft of feather asparagus the florist had included.

"Thank you," she said. "But an artist is only as good as her materials. I couldn't have done it without the lovely flowers. You're very generous."

"I'm also very rich," he said easily, taking the vase from her. "I don't say that to boast, but to let you know in case you were wondering what you'd turned down."

"I wasn't," she said. "I recognized your Beacon Hill address as posh if not downright opulent." What she didn't say was that it was only a block or two from her maternal grandparents' most definitely luxurious mansion, one she had visited exactly once since her parents' deaths.

"But you weren't impressed."

"Not particularly. I earn enough to keep myself comfortable. If I were the type to wear sable, I'd also be the type who wouldn't value it unless I'd earned it myself." She nodded at the vase of flowers he held. "Would you mind setting those on the little corner table by the windows in the living room? And while you're there, you might like to put a match to the fire."

"Yes, ma'am," he said. He was back seconds later, standing too close, taking up more than his fair share of the limited space in the kitchen. "Who are the kids whose picture I had to move to put the flowers on the table?"

She smiled over her shoulder as she filled a large pot with water for boiling the noodles. "My niece and nephew. Roxanne's six and Jason's nearly ten."

"Good looking children, but neither of them is like you at all."

"No. They take after Sharon. She's the one who inherited all the Gypsy blood from our dad's family. Their father had dark hair, too, so maybe that helped."

"Had?"

She twisted her mouth sideways. "All right. Has. Unless he's been run over by a bus sometime in the last three years, or shot or strangled or otherwise met his just deserts."

"You aren't fond of your brother-in-law."

"Ex-brother-in-law," she said, and thumped the pot onto the stove, then slapped a lid on it.

Max had the good sense to recognize that she had also slapped a lid on the topic of discussion. "Smells good," he said as she stirred sour cream into the already rich meat sauce, then set the dish back into the oven.

"That'll whet your appetite. It'll be another half hour or so, if you'd like a drink."

"Show me where and tell me what, and I'll tend bar. You take off that apron so I can whet my appetite on the dress you're wearing as well as the aromas from the kitchen."

Sliding an arm around her shoulders, he led her into the living room, then turned her and untied her apron himself. "Oh, those appetites you arouse in me," he whispered in her ear.

"I . . . thought it was the scent of the food that was going to whet your appetite," she whispered, feeling the heat of his breath across her cheek as his mouth approached hers.

His blue eyes were half-closed, just tiny, glittering slices of indigo between thick, black lashes. Even so, she saw the laughter in them. "So I lied. I missed you, Jeanie. I need to kiss you."

"You saw me only five or six hours ago." She needed to kiss him, too, but was enjoying the anticipation too much to want to hurry. She touched his lips with her fingertips, holding him off. "And you kissed me then. When do you get enough, Mr. McKenzie?"

"Start kissing me and don't stop until I tell you," he said in a rough, yet quiet voice, his fingers touching each of the tiny covered buttons that marched down the back of her red dress from neckline to the narrow gold belt at her waist. He wasn't undoing them, or even trying to. He was merely toying with them, maybe counting them for future reference, she thought. Another of those delicious little thrills he was capable of inducing raced right along under those very buttons. "Then you'll know it's enough." His moving lips slid down her fingers to her palm. The tip of his tongue pressed insinuatingly against her skin, then moved into a groove between two fingers while his gaze held hers. "Your eyes go all silver and shiny when I do that," he whispered huskily. "There's something in their depths that moves like smoke from a campfire rising against a winter sky. It makes me feel hot and primitive and so full of wanting that I could take you right here on the living room floor."

She drew in a sharp breath that did nothing to alleviate the sudden stab of exquisite physical pain that struck her deep inside. "Max . . . stop . . . saying those things."

"Then kiss me so I can't talk."

She smiled, sliding her hand around the back of his head, his dark curls wrapping around her fingers. "I guess that's the best solution, isn't it?"

"The only one," he agreed, and covered her mouth with his, hard and hot and wet and full-blown like one of his roses. It was the kind of kiss she knew she had been born to share in. It was full of his taste, full of his scent, full of his power. It answered something in her that was just as full-blown, just as potent, just as needful. Their tongues met and moved together. Small, glad sounds came from two throats. Two pairs of hands explored muscle and skin and shapes and textures, and two hearts hammered in rapid unison. It was a voluptuous kiss, laden with portent, demanding a deeper penetration than a mere tongue into a hot, wet mouth. It was a kiss that should have been shared by two naked people already in bed, intending it to be a mere preliminary to what their bodies both cried out for in ever-increasing intensity.

"Max . . ." Jeanie pulled away first, leaning her forehead against his chest. "Lord, I . . . Oh, Max!" Her breath came in great, heaving gasps. She rolled her head back and forth, trying to clear it of the reeling dizziness their kisses had created.

"I know. I know." His hands trembled on her back. She felt his legs shaking against hers. "How the hell can something like that happen so fast, each and every time we touch?"

"It has to stop. That's all there is to it. Or we'll never get any dinner."

He dragged her face up to stare down into her eyes. "Do I look as if I care?"

She shook her head. "But you should. I invited you for dinner, Max. Not for . . . anything else."

"I know that. I knew it when you asked me." Gently, he released her. "And Jeanie, believe me, that's all I came for."

"Whew!" She blew a breath of air up over her face. "Well, I must confess I'm glad someone was sure of what I meant when I invited you. Because I sure as heck wasn't."

He laughed softly. "I really like your truthfulness, Jeanie Leslie. Among other, er . . . attributes. Now, let's get that drink you offered me before I forget everything my mother taught me about being a gentleman. I need it."

"The drink or the lessons?"

"Both."

In the living room, he poured her the glass of burgundy she asked for and a straight rye for himself, then sat down opposite her, taking the wing chair rather than joining her on the sofa.

She sipped. He took a hefty slug, then set the glass on a leather coaster. "Listen," he said, looking not at her but into the dancing flames in the fireplace. They highlighted the planes and angles of his face, shadowing his eyes, gilding the tips of his lashes and the touches of gray at his temples. "You're right. What's going on between us does have to stop. Or at least slow down, unless you're willing to give me what I want from you . . ." He looked at her now, his expression serious, his mouth a firm straight line with a tight band of pale skin around it. ". . . and that's not simply sex, as great as I know it's going to be.

"Max, I—"

"No. Please, let me finish. I want more from you than a quick roll, Jeanie. And I know you're not the kind of woman to give a man that anyway, so what flares up between us whenever we're together isn't fair to you."

"You mean you realize you might tempt me toward immoral actions?"

"You're laughing at me," he accused, looking rueful.

"Only a little. I'm grateful for your consideration, Max. I want you to know that. And you're right. I don't have casual affairs. And I don't want one. As wonderful as I know making love would be with you." At least she didn't think she did, but after a few more kisses like the ones they'd shared, she could very easily change her mind.

"Of course I'm right. And I don't want any more casual affairs either. I've had enough of those to last a couple of lifetimes. I want permanency, marriage, and I want it with you. So, until you can agree to my terms, we'll cool the heated embraces."

"I'm not going to agree to those terms. I don't want marriage, Max. It would be all wrong for me under the circumstances."

"And those are?"

"That I don't love you. That you don't love me. That you believe there's no such thing as love. I happen to disagree. I think that it does exist, but since it doesn't between us, then I won't marry you."

"If you thought you loved me, would you?"

She noticed he didn't say "If I loved you," or even "if you thought I loved you," and it was a telling omission. He wasn't kidding when he said he didn't believe in love.

"No, I wouldn't. One-sided love would be as bad as no love at all." That much she knew from her sister's experience. Besides, she didn't think she could bring herself to take that step even if they were both in love with each other. It just wasn't in her plans for the future.

"I'm glad you see it that way. One of the things I hate most is having to hurt women who think they're in love with me, when there is no way in the world I can return that depth of emotion."

She nodded, wondering if her disappointment showed. What was the matter with her, anyway? Was she one of those horrible women who liked the idea of a man falling for her even when she wasn't in love with him herself? She frowned slightly. She didn't think she was one. But it still rankled that a man could want her as much as he claimed to and not profess some kind of affection. Although, she recalled, he had said that he cared, that he'd felt some kind of primitive, possessive anger when that man in the garage had touched her. Cared? What did that mean? To him? To her? She wished for wisdom she didn't possess.

"Fine," she said, getting to her feet. "Then we're in complete agreement. I'll finish getting dinner ready. Help yourself to another drink and put more wood on the fire if it needs it."

She might know he was right, but it hurt nonetheless to have him say it. He wanted marriage; she did not. Impasse. And to him impasse meant no more wild kisses, no more fiery embraces, no chance that one of those embraces would carry them right over the edge and into the kind of relationship he no longer wanted with a woman unless he had her tied up in bonds so tight there'd be no escaping. So, she would feed him his dinner, wish him a friendly good night, and send him on his way. From this moment on, their relationship would be one of casual business acquaintances, and that, she decided, vigorously stirring noodles that should have been treated gently, was going to be that.

"Right," she said briskly after the dinner dishes had been cleared away from the small, gateleg table in the living room. She wished she hadn't had that second glass of wine. It made it more difficult to force her mind to business. "You brought the letter for my client?"

"Yes." He reached into the inside breast pocket

of his light gray suit jacket and pulled out a neatly folded paper. "I'll read it for you."

"No!" She felt herself flush as she yelped out the word, but some traitorous part of her curled and twisted pleasurably at the thought of actually hearing his voice read the words. She wouldn't be able to stand it. "That won't be necessary," she said quickly. "As long as it's handwritten and you've followed the guidelines set out by the client, I'm certain it'll be fine. I'll just send it out in the morning." She reached out her hand for it, but he withheld it.

"You might not be able to read my writing."

"If I can't, then the client won't be able to either," she said with dismay. "Your writing can't be that bad."

"Wanna bet? See for yourself."

She groaned as she tried to decipher his impossible scribble. It was illegible. "Max, you have to do better than this! Didn't you learn the McLean's Method of writing in school? I thought it was an absolute in every curriculum in the entire country."

"I did, but my mind works faster than my fingers can go, so when I write, I scribble. The only person who can read it is Freda."

Jeanie felt her eyes widen as the thought crossed her mind that if that were the case, then Freda had definitely read the first letter Max had sent. "Oh, my Lord . . ." she whispered.

He laughed, reading her mind again. "No, she didn't type that one for me. I can type, you know. I do all of my work directly on a word processor. Freda just guards my gates and does the research and scut work."

She breathed a sigh of relief. "Well, you're just

going to have to slow down your mind as well as your hand and do this letter over again."

She walked to the desk in the corner of the living room, pulling out a drawer and laying a pad of notepaper on top with a pen. "Here, sit down. It won't take you long, I'm sure."

"No," he said cheerfully, "not long at all. Well, maybe longer than usual, because I'll have to try to write carefully and slowly and legibly. But you can put up with my presence another hour or so, can't you?"

She agreed that she could. "I'll do the dishes while you work."

"No. No, stay and keep me company. It'll go easier if I can look up and see your face now and then." He smiled that smile she could never turn away from. "Inspiration, Jeanie."

"I don't suppose you'll need it. After all, you're a professional, aren't you? Don't words just come naturally to your mind?"

His smile turned into a grin. "Not always. And certain inspiration does have its place. So sit where I can see you. Please?"

She told herself she'd do it because she wanted the damned letter written. She could load the dishwasher later, just as she'd intended all along. She hated people who insisted on cleaning up their kitchens while their guests languished in the living room or felt obliged to help.

Max sat down, angled the paper before him, and picked up the pen. For the first time she noticed he was left-handed. She wondered why she hadn't seen it before. After all, they'd shared two lunches and a late-night snack, plus dinner. Probably during those times she'd been too busy trying to keep her mind from skittering off on little side trips into fantasyland. And at dinner all she'd been aware of was the way his eyes had shone in the light of the candles she'd been rash enough to set on the table between them.

" 'Dearest,' " he said aloud as he wrote. " 'Tonight was the most wonderful evening I've spent. To be with you, to touch you, kiss you, look into your eyes through the gleam of candlelight and see the light reflected there, all silver and shining, thrilled me . . .' " He looked up. "Thrilled me how? What do you think?"

"You're writing this, not me." Jeanie leafed through a magazine, pretending to read. So he'd noticed her eyes through the candlelight had he?

" '. . . thrilled me right through to my soul. The smoky gray' . . . oops . . . listen, Jeanie, will it be okay if I have to scratch things out? I'll have to totally obliterate that. I meant to write velvety brown, like the guy said, but I was getting carried away and . . ."

"Go ahead. Scratch things out if you have to. Maybe it'll make the damned letter look more spontaneous."

He looked up sharply at her tone. "You sound grouchy. Are you tired? Would you like me to take this home and finish it? I could have it in your office by nine."

"No. It's okay." She realized she had sounded churlish, and it wasn't fair. After all, he was trying to do a job to please one of her clients. It was good for her business for him to do the job properly. "Just go ahead and write. But do you have to read it out loud as you're doing it?"

"It helps to slow me down, but I won't if it . . . bothers you," he said with a smile that was too knowing.

"I'm trying to read a very interesting article, is all," she said, hoping he wouldn't ask what the article was about. How could she explain a sudden vital desire to know more about the dry-land windsurfing simulator being used to train Olympic-class board sailors?

"I'll speak quietly," he promised, and she strained to hear his murmured words.

" 'How many years we've wasted, you and I, never knowing the' . . . um, let's see, the . . . 'magic we could create together.' Yeah, that's good. Magic's the term, all right. 'But now that we know, we'll waste no more. I'll come to you, my angel, sweep you into my arms and slowly, so very slowly, strip away all the physical barriers that separate us. I'll enfold you in my arms, press my hungry mouth to your breasts. You'll wrap your silken thighs around my hips, your arms about my neck, and as the heat builds between us, we'll begin a fantastic climb, higher and higher. We'll gaze at each other until our sight blurs, our hearing is filled with only the rush of each other's breathing, and our every sense is captured by the passion flaring between us, building to such heights it can do nothing but burst in a shower of golden lights and fanfare of blaring trumpets. And then, slowly, slowly, we'll begin again and—' "

"Dammit, Max! Stop it! That's not a love letter. It's a script for an obscene phone call! What happened to romantic walks in the moonlight, holding hands, and comparing dreams? What about long talks by the fireside? Can't you write about leisurely dinners in fine restaurants with unobtrusive waiters and strolling violinists? Read the guidelines, for heaven's sake!"

"He doesn't say they've actually done any of those things. Just that he'd like to do them with her. I haven't got to that part yet, is all. I'm embellishing as he suggested, adding things I'd like to do with a woman." His direct gaze told her exactly with which woman he'd like to do those things.

"Well, that's enough! Go home! Finish the wretched thing in your own place. Write it on your word processor, then copy it out longhand. Just remember to do it slowly and neatly and have it on my desk by nine in the morning."

"Yeah. I think that'd be best." He got to his feet, folded the original and his new copy, and slid them into his breast pocket, then pulled her to her feet. "At this rate, it might take me all night to finish, and I can see you're really tired. You need to get to bed."

She tugged her hand out of his warm clasp and stepped away from him. She didn't even want to think about the word bed with him still in her apartment.

"Fine," she said. "Good night."

"Yup," he said, heading to the door. "You too." He picked up his coat and shrugged into it. "Sleep tight," he said, and left.

"Not even a little kiss, Grandma Margaret. Not even a tiny peck on the cheek, on the forehead, not even a handshake, for heaven's sake. Oh, I know he's right to cool it, but did he have to cool it so fast? Put it into such a damned deep freeze that there can't even be a little bit of warmth between us again?"

Suddenly, to her horror, Jeanie burst into tears of rage and frustration and good, old-fashioned hurt feelings. "What am I going to do, Grandma? I think I'm falling in love with the man!"

Through the sounds of her own crying, she heard the gentle tinkle of golden bangles, but found very little comfort in the musical tones. What she wanted was the loud, sweet fanfare of a golden trumpet heralding some kind of a miracle.

Seven

Max was just coming out of the elevator at eight forty-five the next morning as Jeanie opened the door from the stairwell. They both stopped and stared at each other, she wondering if her newly discovered love would show. She loved him and hated herself for that weakness. If he knew, if he pitied her, she couldn't stand it. Then slowly he smiled, and she realized that it wasn't written in neon across her forehead: *Here is another stupid woman who has fallen in love with Max McKenzie.* "Hi," he said. "Do you always take the stairs?"

"Yes."

"Even in your apartment? All the way to the fifth floor?"

"Like I told you before. Exercise is good for the body."

He touched her hair, careful not to muss its neat appearance, then let his caress trail down over her cheek. She stood absolutely still, hoping not to give herself away by the ready response of her body to his touch. "Maybe it's good for your body, but mine, after a lousy night, needs all the help it can get. I didn't sleep much after I left you."

She unlocked her outer office door, turned on the lights, and opened the door to her private office. "I didn't, either. Too much coffee, I guess."

"On you, it doesn't show."

"Thanks." She opened a drawer and dropped her purse inside. "You lie nicely, Mr. McKenzie."

"It wasn't coffee that kept me awake. It was guilt."

She turned and looked at him. *He knew?* "Guilt? Over what?"

"Over what I did. With that letter. It wasn't very nice. I apologize."

"What you did?"

"I was deliberately teasing you. Trying to make you change your mind. Using sex to get my way." He swallowed hard, reached into his pocket, and handed her a sheaf of papers. "I did the letter correctly, plus a few more just to keep a couple of days ahead of the game. Read them if you like. There's nothing . . . objectionable in them."

She knew she couldn't bear to read them. She knew if she did, she'd fall apart inside, and beg him to at least try to love her. "I trust you." She took them and, without even glancing at them, stuffed them into an envelope already addressed to the box number they were meant for. Then she sealed it and laid it down again.

"Thank you, Max. It was good of you to get them here so early. I'm sure you have a lot to do and so d—" She broke off and jerked around at the sound of the sharp ring of the phone on her desk. "Excuse me. That's my private line."

He watched as she listened. He could make out hysterical feminine tones but not the words. As Jeanie's face whitened and she swayed, he leapt forward and shoved her chair under her, forcing her to sit. He kept his hands tightly on her shoulders, standing behind her, listening to her end of the conversation.

"He never got there? Sharon, it's just across the field and a mile along the trail! I know, I know. I'm sorry. Of course you've been telling yourself that ever since you heard. No! Listen. It is not your fault! He's nearly ten years old, and he's walked to Mark's house hundreds of times, spent the night there hundreds of times. You had no way of knowing that this once Mark's mother didn't know the boys' plans. Sharon, please! Please stop saying it's your fault! Okay, okay, I'd blame myself too. I know. I'm on my way. We'll find him, Sharon. I know it's crazy to say don't worry, because I'm worried as hell myself, but I'm coming and we'll find him. You just hang onto Roxy and wait for me. I'll be with you as fast as I can get there. In the meantime, tell the police every little thing you can think of, check with all his other friends, and try to stay calm for Roxy's sake. I love you, Sharon. I'm coming."

She slammed the phone down and stood up. Shrugging off Max's hands, she looked blindly around her office as if not knowing what she needed. She shook her head. "Jason's missing. Sharon said he asked if he could spend the night with a friend. When he didn't show up at school this morning, the principal phoned to see where he was. They always do that if the parents don't call, and Sharon called Mark's mom who said she hadn't seen him and that Mark hadn't said Jason was coming. Mark hasn't seen him since yesterday at school! He's been out all night!"

Jeanie broke down, buried her face in her hands and cried. "Oh, Lord, he's only ten, and it's so cold at night!"

She stared distractedly around, tears running down her face. "The police have started a search. I have to go help. Where are my car keys?"

Max opened the drawer and took out her purse. He slid the strap over her shoulder and wrapped an arm around her. Gently, he steered her into the outer office where Cindy was just turning on her typewriter. "There are some papers on Ms. Leslie's desk. Get them out right away, will you? There's a family emergency. Cancel all her appointments until further notice. She'll be in touch when she can. You can hold the fort, can't you?"

"Yes, sir. I sure can. Can I help?"

"No. I'll look after Ms. Leslie. You look after the office."

He shoved Jeanie through the elevator doors even though she balked. "No! The stairs! Please, I can't . . ." But it was too late. The doors slid shut. She stood rigid, beads of sweat breaking out on her face, her fists clenched at her sides, her eyes wide, her breathing shallow and panicked. Max stared at her.

"You're claustrophobic! So that explains your stair fetish."

She couldn't reply, only stared at the numbers as they slowly went from three to two to one, until the doors finally hissed open. "Oh, sweetheart, I'm sorry to have put you through that on top of everything else. But come on, that ordeal's over now. My car's right out here."

"No! I'll take mine. This isn't your . . ."

He shoved open the main doors of the building, opened the passenger side of his car, and put her on the seat. In very few long strides, he was around, behind the wheel, and pulling away from the curb. "Your problems are my problems, Jeanie. That's the way it is." He drove quickly but was always in control. In no time at all they were in front of her apartment building. "Inside," he said briskly. "Get into warm clothes, strong shoes, whatever else you'll need to join in the search."

"There's no time! I have to get to Sharon. I'll find some clothes in Nanaimo. I can stuff myself into her jeans, if I don't do up the button."

"It'll take less time if you quit arguing with me. You'll need your own shoes, at least. Move, Jeanie. Now!" He reached across her, opened the door, and shoved her out. "Pack extra socks, shoes, pants. If you don't have a backpack, put them in a bag. We can add them to mine when I come back for you."

"But where—"

He didn't wait for her to ask where he was going, just peeled away from the curb. She could see he was already talking into his cellular phone. She ran for her building's front door, up the stairs, into her apartment, and was stripping off her business dress even as she slammed the door. She did not have a backpack, but for some reason did exactly as he had said. She dressed herself warmly, then stuffed a complete change of clothing into a bag, dragged on her thigh-length down jacket, dug out a pair of ski gloves and a red woolen hat, and was ready. How had he known that she wouldn't just be able to sit and comfort Sharon while others searched, that she would need to be out there in the thick of it herself? It was uncanny the way he'd read her, when he knew her so short a time.

In the kitchen, she stuffed a bag of raisins, another of chocolate chips, and one of blanched almonds down the sides of the bag, thought a bit, then added some dried apricots, and a bag of mints. If she was going to be beating the woods in search of her precious nephew, she was not going to waste time going back to some checkpoint for food. She had just made her way down the stairs when Max pulled up in front of her apartment building, reached over, and flung open the door for her.

He pulled a U-turn, and she groaned. "No! The other way's quickest to get to the freeway."

"Relax, honey. We're flying. It's all arranged. My chopper's getting wound up now, flight plan's being filed, weather checked, and in minutes we'll be in Nanaimo, where a car will be waiting for us—unless there's room to land at your sister's place? I'll need an open area at least fifty feet wide, with no electric wires or anything like that in the way. And good, solid ground. But no school yards, either, or playing fields where there might be people. Know of any place like that?"

"Helicopter? Max, don't you understand? This is a little boy we're looking for! A little boy who's probably lost in dense woods, not a ship at sea! A helicopter will be useless. Thank you, but this is going to be a ground search!"

"Jeanie, I know that. I'm a member of PEP."

"PEP?" It sound familiar, but she couldn't place it.

"Provincial Emergency Program. The helicopter is just to get us there ten times quicker than driving will. Now, is there some place safe we can land, or do I go to the airport?"

"There's a big field right behind our house. It's fenced because Roxy had to be kept in when they first came home. She was only three. Jason played there too. So did Sharon and I as little children." She choked up. Why couldn't Jason have stayed small enough to be kept in that big, safe fenced field?

"Easy, now. We'll find him, Jeanie. There'll be lots of searchers. He will be found. Believe me. Trust me."

She controlled her emotions, fighting back the tears that had threatened to overcome her. "Thank you, Max. How can I ever thank you for all this?"

"You can reach into the backseat and grab that empty pack there beside mine. Start stuffing your things into it. It'll save time and there won't be room in the chopper to do it."

By the time she had the smaller of the two backpacks crammed with what she'd brought, they were at the private airport where Max kept his helicopter. It was a tiny machine, just big enough for the two of them and their gear. Its rotors already were whirling overhead. Pressing her into a crouch, he shunted her into the left-hand seat, buckled her into a complicated set of crossed straps, tightened them, then ran around to replace the man who was at the controls. She could see but not hear the two men speaking, and then Max was pulling on a set of headphones, slamming his door, slipping into his own harness, and reaching for the controls, which he manipulated with both hands and both feet. The copter tilted, nose down, as they lifted rapidly and skimmed over the tops of a bank of trees at the far end of the strip.

Tapping another set of headphones hanging on the side of her seat, he indicated she should put them on. His voice came across clearly. "Press the little button on the floor when you want to talk. The one marked Intercom Switch. You're going to have to give me directions to your sister's house."

She nodded her understanding, but he was busy speaking to someone on the ground. She had nothing to tell him yet. He was headed in the right direction. It would have been an exciting trip if she hadn't been so terrified for her nephew, so concerned for her sister. The trip seemed to drag on unbearably, but in actuality it was only minutes before the skyline of Nanaimo appeared.

"Go that way," she said, pointing toward the hills behind the city.

"I didn't hear you. Press the button."

She did as she was told and repeated her instructions, pointing again.

"Give me a landmark to aim at."

"The middle gap in the ridge behind that tall church steeple. That's where the road goes that leads home. I don't know any other way than by road." Her voice wobbled, and she felt less than helpful.

"That's okay," he said. "I don't expect you to know any other way. We'll follow your road. Just warn me about two minutes before we get to where you want me to land."

"There's the roof of the house," she said moments later. "See it? Dark red tiles, two wings coming off the main section?"

"Got it," he said, and she remembered the horrendous cost of having those tiles put on not six months before. She hoped the helicopter wouldn't blow them off, but if it meant finding Jason more quickly, then she'd replace each one herself, gladly.

"The field is the one just behind it."

"Right," he said, and then was speaking again to someone else about what he was doing and where he was about to do it. As the roof of the house went by under them, Jeanie recalled the first dream in which the man who looked like Max had appeared. In the dream, she had been coming home during a storm, cresting the hill in the road, on foot for some reason, when she saw Sharon on the roof trying to hold on the old, silvered cedar shakes that were blowing away. The dream man had come up the drive behind her on a horse, scooped her onto the animal with him, and galloped to Sharon's rescue. He'd been wearing a black cloak and had flown, cloak billowing, to the roof, where he plucked Sharon to safety, waved a magic hand and restored the shakes. The storm had stopped as if by the same magic, and then the man had been gone.

Jeanie had laughed about it, put it down to the fact that she'd taken her niece and nephew to see *Batman* the night before, and that she and Sharon had been discussing the cost of having the leaky roof repaired or replaced.

Yet, he had continued to occur in dreams for many months, always coming to Sharon's rescue, and now, Jeanie thought, as he set the helicopter down neatly at the edge of the field near the house, there he was, doing it again. But this time he was to rescue Sharon's son. As the sound of the rotors wound down and Max lifted off her headphones, she looked into his eyes. He wasn't there to be a hero for Sharon. He was there for one reason only: Because she needed him.

Leaning over the couple of inches her tight straps permitted, she kissed him hard on the mouth. "Thank you," she said. "You're a very special guy."

"Yes, sir." Max was speaking to the Royal Canadian Mounted Police Officer in charge of the search coordination. "I'm with the PEP group in Victoria. I'm a friend of the family." Max looked over at where Jeanie held her weeping sister and niece close. "The boy's aunt and I have come prepared to search. We'll put ourselves at your disposal. Instructions?"

"Maybe the girl should stay with her sister."

"Maybe she should, but she won't. Believe me. I know her. Besides, she grew up here. She knows the area perhaps better than most, knows what might tempt a kid off the normal trail to his friend's house. She might be able to figure out what could have fascinated him so much that he lied about going to the friend's house in the first place. She is also with PEP," he said with a completely straight face. "We work well together as a team. Can you assign us an area?"

"If the boy's aunt knows the immediate area, then that's what she should concentrate on. It was gone over first, of course, the entire trail and a hundred feet or so to each side of it. The search commenced right after the mother called, even though we feel we have to treat this as a runaway, in spite of the kid's age. He did clearly state that he was invited to spend the night with his friend. His mother's blaming herself, poor woman.

"We are also not discounting kidnapping," the policeman said. "The father's whereabouts are unknown, except that he's believed to be in Europe. Interpol has been advised and are trying to locate him."

"Lord! I don't think that's occurred to Jeanie. Has the mother mentioned it?"

"No, but we mentioned it to her. She doesn't believe it's possible. She is convinced the boy is lost, pure and simple, that he expected to get permission to spend the night with his friend when he got there."

"Well, he's a ten year old." Max shook his head. "It sounds reasonable, I guess."

"I think so, too, but we have to take everything into account. In the interim, several teams have combed the woods just back of here, but they'll have moved further out by now. Those woods are full of gullies and tangles of deadfalls and Lord knows how many places a kid could be lost. He could even be bushed."

Max nodded. "You mean have convinced himself that everything he sees, including a rescuer, is a danger to him?"

"That's it. Maybe if he hears his aunt's voice, he'll respond."

"Right. Has the area been taped?"

"Every fifteen feet. But at this stage, and in this terrain, even taping doesn't always mean the ground has been thoroughly searched. If he's unconscious, as he could well be after a night with the temperature down to about seven Celsius, unless he managed to keep moving, he's going to be hard to see. He's wearing a red down jacket with a hood and warm jeans. And at least it was a dry night, so we're hoping he isn't suffering too badly from hypothermia. And one more thing we have to consider, Mr. McKenzie"—the cop paused as if not wanting to go into it but knowing he must—"the area, indeed the entire damned city, is riddled underneath with old coal mine shafts. Most of the entrances to them have been located and sealed, but new ones are always cropping up after each of the frequent little earth tremors the whole coast gets. All the teams have been warned to be extremely cautious. I'm warning you too; watch where you put your feet."

"Okay." Max nodded. Jeanie, her pack already riding high on her back, was coming toward him, her face pale and her mouth taut.

"You sure you don't want to stay with your sister?" he asked as the police officer moved away to talk to another group who were just stepping out of the back of a large bakery van.

"I'm sure. She understands. She wants me to go out. She . . . oh, Max, she believes *I'm* going to find him!" For a moment she came close to breaking down again but thrust her chin high and held onto her composure. He steadied her with his hands on her shoulders. "Max . . . what if I don't?"

"Then someone else will," he said. Taking her arm, he turned her toward the trail Sharon had seen Jason disappear on into the woods. "We're to start here. Every few feet, we stop and you call. We're hoping he'll respond to your voice, if he's gotten so scared he's afraid of everything."

"I understand." Drawing in a deep breath, Jeanie took Max's warm, dry hand in hers and held on for dear life. As they strode into the forest, a light drizzle began to mist the branches of the trees overhead. "Jason!" she called, waited, listened, then called again. "Ja–a–a–son!"

They did the entire path, then moved to the west side, following the line of bright orange surveyor's tapes through the tangled forest, keeping each other in constant sight. Presently, they were joined by three more teams of two, each one taking another line of tapes to follow, each team stopping and waiting after Jeanie called her nephew's name. They probed the thick salal, looked under the low-hanging branches of cedar trees, tore aside small hemlocks to peer under ancient downed trees, and examined the inside of each hollow stump they encountered.

Hours passed. Fine drizzle turned to steady rain. Max pulled bright yellow slickers for both of them out of his pack. The small one belonged to his mother, he said. She had been happy to lend it for the search. The rain eased and then stopped, but the bushes were sodden. They kept the waterproofs on.

Some of the searchers had returned to the control point for hot food and drink and to replenish their supplies of marking tapes. Jeanie refused to leave. She nibbled chocolate chips and almonds. Max made her pause long enough to drink half a cup of brandy-laced coffee from the Thermos in his pack, and then they were on again.

"Jason! Ja–a–a–son!" Her voice was growing so hoarse, she wondered if he'd even recognize it now if he heard it, but she would not give up.

"Jeanie, we have to turn back soon," Max said. "The light will be gone by the time we make our way back to the main trail. And it's starting to rain harder again." Leaving tapes tied to trees every fifteen feet, they were following what might have been a winding, natural trail through the woods, a trail likely made by deer and other animals on their daily forages for food and water, but it interested Jeanie because it might also have been a trail made by a little boy who had played here often over the past three years. Something about it drew her on.

"We both have flashlights," she said, "and the slickers are keeping us dr—" Her sentence broke off as she stopped and stared in dismay when the trail came to a dead end just where a particularly densely leafed branch of cedar swept to the ground.

"No. See? It's petered out." Max's tone held despair, and she knew how hard he had been hoping too.

On the left was a pile of tangled branches and logs, where several trees had blown down together years ago in a storm. No trail went that way. On the right an impassable stand of sharply thorned devil's club barred the way, with a steep, rocky bluff immediately behind it. Jason knew enough about devil's club not to tangle with that particular hazard. Jeanie was about to agree with Max and turn back when she looked again at that thick cedar bough and thought what a perfect shelter it would have made for a little boy lost at night. Underneath, it would be just like a tent. As she lifted it back and peered beyond it, she saw a very distinct path leading away from the far side of the massive trunk. "Max! Look at this."

He crowded in beside her. "What?"

"The trail goes on. See it?" She slipped under

the sweeping cedar bough and began to follow the beaten track.

"Honey, no. Come back." He took her arm. "It's nothing more than a deer trail, and we can't follow it. Besides, we only have one more tape, and you know the rules. We don't go fifteen feet in any direction without leaving a tape."

"I don't think it's just a deer trail. Look, branches have been broken off not eaten off the way they'd be if only deer used it. It might have started out that way but . . . Max . . . look! A sneaker track! Please. Go tie that last tape to the cedar. We have to go on. This might be it. I have a feeling. Please, Max! I can't leave until I know where this trail goes!"

"All right," he said, "but we'll follow it for only a very short distance, Jeanie. Wait here while I tie that tape."

But she couldn't wait. She seemed pulled by a force too strong to withstand, and when the trail ended abruptly against a rock face, she couldn't believe it—until she saw the fissure. Bending, turning on her flashlight, she shone the beam inside and saw a glimpse of bright red. Jason, she knew, was wearing a red ski jacket.

"Max!" she screamed. "He's here!" Then, turning sideways, she slid out of her pack, shoved it in before her, and scrambled into the narrow cave, feeling the terror of claustrophobia begin to claw at her but fighting it down. Jason was more important. He was there. That tiny scrap of red that was probably his down jacket lay so still, she knew he must be asleep or unconscious. She had found him. He was safe! He would be all right! "Jason! Jase . . . baby, it's me, Aunt Jeanie." The passage widened slightly, and the roof of it rose to the point where she could get to her knees. She moved faster now, still shoving her pack ahead of her, and behind her she heard Max calling her name.

"Jeanie! No! Wait for me! Don't go in there! I don't have any more—" but the rest was lost as the narrow fissure around her began to crumble and pebbles peppered her head and shoulders. "Jeanie, come out!" Max shouted, and she looked over her shoulder at his flashlight beam as he followed her in.

"Get out!" he shouted. "Get out Jeanie, it's caving in!"

"I can't! Jason's here! He's hurt! Get help, Max, get help!

But even as she screamed at him, she saw him lunge toward her, his pack a blur that came flying through the beam of dust-filled light. Then he was lying on top of her, and all around them the earth groaned and crumbled, great pieces of it breaking off and thundering into the passage behind. There was thick, choking dust, more showers of sharp pebbles, until finally silence came, silence broken only by the harsh breathing of two terrified human beings and the faint, almost musical tinkle of trickling water.

"Are you hurt?"

Max's voice came from a long distance away.

"No. Are you?"

"My foot's caught. Can you slide ahead, out from under me? Go easy, Jeanie. Shine your light first and see what's there."

What was there was the larger cavern, the small scrap of red that looked like the bent elbow of a sleeve just protruding from behind a rock, and a tiny, glittering creek sliding down a wall to form a little pool close to her extended left hand. She was torn so strongly between wanting to go to that small splotch of red that was so terribly still and wanting to help Max, that she yearned to be able to cut herself into two pieces. Gently, she slid forward, then got to her knees and turned to shine the light back over Max. One of his feet was buried under a pile of what appeared to be small, loose rocks.

"I think I can dig you out," she said, setting her pack aside, struggling to free one of the straps of his pack that was pinned under his hip. Whatever she found when she went to Jason, she was going to need Max. "Let me know if I hurt you."

"I'm not hurt, just stuck."

With her bare hands, she tore at the rocks, and soon his foot was free, having been well protected by his strong leather boot. Jeanie scrambled around the outcrop of rock where the red thing was and let out a cry of utter despair.

"Jeanie, sweetheart, what is it?"

Max caught her around the waist and swung her aside, flashing his light over the site. There, lying on a broad, dusty ledge, was a bright red sleeping bag, the very one she had bought Jason for his ninth birthday nearly a year before. There was a bag of cookies, a can of pork and beans, and stack of comic books sitting nearby.

Of Jason, however, there was no sign at all.

"Come on," she said, scrambling up off her knees. "He's in this cave somewhere! We can find him, Max! He's here! I know it! He must be hurt in one of the other passages. Help me, Max! I have to find him. I must know if he's safe!" One more time, she raised her cracking voice and called out desperately, "Ja–a–a–son!" and was met with nothing more than a hollow echo.

Max held her tightly against him, his flashlight held steady as he turned in a slow circle. "Jeanie, honey, he isn't here. There are no side passages." The light came to stop on the fall of rubble that marked the passage through which they had entered the cavern.

Jeanie felt horror rise up inside her, felt a scream of pure terror building and building even as she battled to hold it within. Her entire body went rigid with terror, and she shook as sweat popped out on her skin. "My Lord! Oh, my Lord, we are in here, and there's no way out!"

Eight

In the beam of his flashlight, Max saw Jeanie's expression of horror, and he held her more tightly. Sweat ran down her face, smearing the dirt encrusting her skin, making small tracks like tears, but she did not weep. "There has to be a way out," she whispered hoarsely, tearing herself free of him, going to the wall behind her nephew's sleeping bag, flashing her beam over it. If there had been a passage there, it was now filled with what appeared to be the same kind of fresh rock fall that blocked the one through which they had entered.

Suddenly, before he realized what she was doing, she began to run, crouched over to avoid the low ceiling of the cavern. She beat at the solid stone with her hands, casting her flashlight beam this way and that, sobbing harshly but without tears. She splashed into the little stream, across the tiny pool and out the other side, and began digging frantically at the loose rubble where Max's foot had been caught. More rock began to fall, a large boulder breaking loose from the wall near her head tumbled into the pool, splashing water over her filthy yellow slicker.

"Jeanie, no. Stop!" He grabbed her and held her, dragging her back to the only part of the cave where he could stand erect. "Take it easy. We'll find a way out. Stop panicking. Sit down for a minute. Rest. Get out of those wet shoes."

She fought him, the terror of being in an enclosed space overwhelming her. She didn't just want to dig. She *needed* to dig! There wasn't enough air. Her breathing was already labored. She struggled against his hold, her eyes wide and unseeing, her mouth agape as she gasped for air she was not getting. Her old horror of suffocation was now the most powerful emotion within her, and she saw Max only as one more obstacle to bar her way. She clawed at his face, kicked at his shins, writhed in his clasp, and continued panting until she was hyperventilating so that she reeled with dizziness.

He stood her away from him, drew back one hand and swung, but let the blow fall short. He could not slap her. Instead he kissed her, holding her head between his hands while she fought him and her fear and the enormity of their circumstances. Finally, when she went limp and leaned against him, he gathered her close and rocked her from side to side, listening to the harshness of her gasps, aching with the need to free her from her terror.

"Jeanie, Jeanie, don't, sweetheart. Listen to me." He spoke slowly and clearly, his voice a quiet benison in the encompassing horror. She leaned back in his arms, looking up at him, focusing on his face, his voice, his calming presence. She clung to it, to all that he represented, forced herself to focus on his words, on the sureness in his tone. "We'll dig ourselves out. But we have to go about it carefully. I know you're scared. I know that you don't think you can get enough air into your lungs, but there is plenty of oxygen in here. Air is coming in at the same place the water does. With air and water, we can survive for a long time. And we have food. Not much, but enough so we can take our time to figure out a plan for digging ourselves out safely. I'm going to let you go now. I'm going to take you back over to Jason's sleeping bag and help you lie down. I want to get you out of that wet slicker and your shoes and socks. You need dry things on. You need a drink from my Thermos. You need to rest for a few minutes, and we both need to think. Okay now? Can I let you go?"

She gulped in a couple of slightly shallower breaths and slowly nodded, her eyes wide and silvery in the light.

Just as slowly, he eased his tight grip on her until he held her only by the upper arms.

"All right?"

"All right," she whispered. "I'm sorry I panicked."

"Don't worry about it. It can happen to anyone." He turned off his flashlight, and she gasped as the value of the light was decreased by fifty percent. Taking her hand, he led her over to the sleeping bag and unsnapped the rain gear that had protected her for so many hours. Setting her flashlight on a rock so its beam reflected off the coal black wall and back into the cavern, he peeled the slicker down over her shoulders and laid it aside. Seating her on the edge of the sleeping bag, he unlaced her wet high tops, tugged them and her wet socks off, then unsnapped his pack and pulled out a warm sweatshirt, which he used as a towel to dry her.

"You'd better get those jeans off, too, and put your dry ones on. When you ran into the pool, you soaked yourself to the knees." Tactfully, he busied himself rummaging through her pack to find her dry jeans, and then handed them to her without looking. He continued to delve into her supplies, to put the dried fruit and candy she'd brought—plus his own trail mix—onto the ledge beside Jason's cookies and beans. When he turned again, she was tugging her sweater down over the waist of her jeans, and her feet were already encased in thick, dry socks. She reached for her spare shoes.

"Here," he said, moments later, having emptied his own pack and taken inventory of what they had. "Drink this." It was more of the hot, sweet coffee laced with brandy. "No, all of it," he said when she handed the cup back to him after having had only a couple of sips. "I'll have mine in a few minutes."

Gratefully, she sipped, and slowly her tremors of fear began to abate. The feeling of tightness remained in her chest, but with concentration she could control the panic that kept rising up. All she had to do was remind herself that they could and would get out. Just as soon as they were able, they were going to start digging. Even with their bare hands, it couldn't take more than a couple of hours to remove the rocks that had fallen into the short passage. But Max was right. They needed rest, and they needed a plan. There was no point in tearing into that pile of rubble and bringing down even more, as she had done. Besides, maybe the other collapsed passage, the one behind her, would be the better bet. They hadn't even examined it yet.

Handing him back the empty cup, she watched him fill it and then sit back, his expression thoughtful. Picking up her flashlight, she shone it toward where the loose rocks lay at the back of the cave, brushed a few pebbles and some dust off the top of the sleeping bag, and glanced over her shoulder at Max. "This looks like smaller stuff, don't you think? Maybe we should start digging here."

He shook his head. "We don't know where that goes, or even if there is a passage there at all. At least with the other one, we're certain it leads outside."

That was true. She went back to the other end of the sleeping bag.

"Jeanie, come here," he said. "Bring the light."

She sat beside him on his folded jacket and felt him wrap his arm around her shoulder. "Honey, I know you're not going to like it, but we'll have to turn off the light. We need to conserve the batteries for when we're digging. When we're not, I'm afraid we won't be able to use it." He took it from her hand, tightened his grip on her, and plunged them into the most profound darkness she had ever experienced. It was even darker than the closet in her grandfather's basement. A low, ululating moan issued from her throat, and she felt renewed fingers of panic tear at her control.

"Please," she whispered in a choked voice. "Please, turn it on!"

"It's all right," said Max. "I'm right here. I'm holding you. You are safe. Put your hand on my chest. Can you feel me breathing? Breathe with me. Slow and steady. You can do it, sweetheart. Just let yourself rise up over the fear. You're in a helicopter. The fear is on the ground. You're lifting high, high above it. It's getting smaller and smaller and smaller, and now we're moving away from it, leaving it behind. We'll never be going back to that place, so it will never be able to get you again." Slowly, as his voice went on and on, the tension began to seep out of her. For many long minutes he talked, his voice ever calm and quiet, and finally she was able to breathe easily. She pulled slightly away from him.

"I guess it's . . . a good thing I'm not afraid of heights too," she said, "since it took a helicopter to fly me up and away from my fear." Her laughter held more than just a hint of tears, but she swallowed them back. They were in this mess because she had led the way into the cave. It was up to her to be a help to Max, not a hindrance. She would control herself. She would learn to conquer her fear.

He gave her a little squeeze, a reward for trying to find humor in what must be the most dreadful situation she'd ever found herself in. Her respirations began to grow choppy once more, and he stroked her back with his hand. "That's right, keep breathing with me. Slowly, Jeanie. Quietly. Softly. There is lots of air in here. I can feel a draft on my face. Lean forward slightly. There, can you feel it? It's cool. It should be against your left cheek. When the light was on, you could see that little space above the water where the stream enters. Remember that it's there. Remember that it's where the air comes from. It doesn't take a big gap for a lot of air to enter. Concentrate on it. Think about it. Can you feel it?"

"I can feel it. I know it's there, Max. I know there's air even without seeing the place where it comes in. It's the child in me that doesn't quite believe that the cracks around the closet door will let in enough."

"The closet?"

"It was in my grandparent's basement. He—my grandfather—put me in there if I was bad."

"I thought you said your sister raised you."

"After our parents died, she did. This was before, when I was very little. My parents used to leave us with them sometimes before . . . before they knew what he did to me. He's my mother's father. I look just like her, and he really doesn't like me much at all. When I was really small, he actually hated me, I think. I also think he believed that if he could teach me right from wrong, I'd turn out better than my mother did. So every time we had to stay there, he 'disciplined' me by locking me in that closet."

"Lord!" Max's disgust was clear, even in the total darkness. "Why didn't your grandmother stop him?"

She sighed. "What could she do? She was his wife. He got to make the rules. You know that old garbage—love, honor, and obey? This world we live in takes it seriously, even now that most women have stopped making that promise and most men claim to have stopped expecting it. My grandmother used to tell me that if I'd just pay attention to what Grandpa wanted and do what I was told, it wouldn't happen. But it always did, somehow. I could never figure out what he wanted of me. I know now what he wanted was to punish my mother for having run off and married a man she loved, rather than the one he had chosen for her. You see, my father was a musician, and that wasn't good enough for him. He thought my father was feckless and, in a way, I guess he was. He and my mother died leaving their children only a house, which Sharon rented out to help defray our living costs while she went to the conservatory on a scholarship.

"Our grandfather, who could have helped, wouldn't. But we didn't care. We were so grateful that Mom and Dad had made Sharon my guardian in the event that they died, instead of our grandparents." Her voice trembled. "I'd have run away rather than live in his house with that awful, dark closet, and . . . do you feel rested enough to start digging now?"

The abrupt change of subject startled him, although he realized it shouldn't have. Jeanie might have been talking of her childhood, but the closest thing to the surface of her consciousness right now was getting out of this dark cave. He turned on the light.

She blinked in the sudden brightness, and the smile on her face was one of pure relief. He wished he didn't have to conserve the batteries, but he really had no idea how long it was going to take to get them out.

"Here," he said, handing her the flashlight. "Find a place where this will shine on the fall, and then get yourself in position to take the junk I pass back to you."

Carefully, slowly, he lifted out the boulder that had come close to crushing her shoulder when she had first begun to dig. A small flutter of pebbles came from the walls by his head. One by one, he removed other rocks, some large, some small, and either passed or rolled them back to her where she disposed of them in a small depression in the wall. An hour passed, and yet another; the small depression was filled, and she had begun to stack rocks and rubble wherever it looked as if it wouldn't be in their way. Max soon suffered from bloody, torn fingers and nails. Jeanie's knees ached from kneeling and crawling, her shoulders burned from lifting and shoving rocks. But in her leather ski gloves, her hands were more protected that his. She wished the gloves would fit him, but his hands were much too large. She could almost feel his pain each time he lifted another piece of rock, and though they had worked without ceasing for what seemed like days, they were no closer to clearing a passage than when they had begun. What had happened, she wondered, to her original estimate of two hours to freedom?

They stopped finally at Max's insistence; she washed his bleeding hands and both their filthy faces in the cold water of the stream, used Max's knife to open Jason's can of beans, and fed both of them. They each had one cookie after the meal.

"Put my other socks on your hands," Jeanie suggested, looking at Max's tattered and bleeding fingers. He was doing the most of the work, taking the brunt of the punishment. The more protection he could get, the easier it would be on him. "It can't hurt, and it might help." But within twenty minutes, her socks were as full of gashes as his skin and were simply getting in the way.

"Max . . . what time is it?" Jeanie slumped back in exhaustion, staring at his back in the now dimming light. She knew many more hours had passed and that her flashlight was almost as spent as they were.

Wearily, he scrunched himself around and held his watch before the flashlight. He blinked, looked again, and said, "Two twenty-eight."

"In the morning?"

"In the morning."

"Then we stop for the night," she said with as much decisiveness as her weariness permitted. "And Max, we may be digging for nothing, you know. When we don't show up, they're going to be looking for us. And when they find that tape you put on the cedar tree, with no trail leading away from it, they'll do what we did and look under the branches. They'll follow the rest of the trail, see the rock fall, and be digging from the other side. But that won't happen till daylight."

"You're right," he said, crawling to the stream and cleaning himself up as best he could. Glancing sideways at Jeanie, he wondered if he should tell her that the chances of anyone's finding the rock fall were remote. *No,* he decided, opening up the sleeping bag to its full width, lying down, and pulling his blanket over them, *there may never be a need for her to know that I didn't have a tape to tie to that cedar bough.* In the inky blackness of the cavern, he felt her shivers of fear, her raspy, panicky breaths. He stroked her back with long, rhythmic massages, whispering to her all the comforting words he could find in his vocabulary. Presently, she slept, and Max relaxed, allowing sleep to overcome him.

The next day was going to be just as hard.

* * *

"This isn't going to be the piece of cake we thought it was, is it?" Jeanie asked sometime during the next day. They had both been wide awake after only five hours sleep and were on their third rest-and-cookie break. The first time Max had called it that she had giggled so much, he'd feared he might have to actually smack her to snap her out of hysteria, but she'd sobered when he clamped her arms in his large, dirty hands.

"You sounded l–like a kindergarten teacher." After allowing her a couple more sobbing laughs, he drew her against his chest, stroking her filthy, tangled hair back from her face.

Her flashlight had lost its last bit of power a few minutes before. They sat sipping water, he from the bean can, she from the thermos cup, and munching their cookies in the dark.

"I wonder if they've found our cedar tree yet? Would we be able to hear them digging if they were out there?" she asked.

"I doubt it," he said, because he doubted anyone was out there digging.

"I bet they've found Jason by now, though," she said, and he murmured agreement because he knew she needed to believe that. "Poor Sharon. This is a rotten thing to do to her, isn't it? She's relied on me so much these past few years, and now I've gone and pulled a lousy, stupid stunt like this." He rocked her slightly, careful not to slop her water.

"Max?"

"I'm right here," he said.

"Hmmm. I know. And I'm glad. But I've been wondering why you dove into the fissure after me when it started to collapse. I know you could have got out. You could have led them to me. You didn't have to put yourself in this position along with me."

He was silent for several moments, then she felt him shrug. "I couldn't let you get sealed into a cave all by yourself. I saw what just being in a lighted elevator had done to you." And he hadn't known whether she might actually have discovered her nephew, injured . . . or worse.

"Oh." She swallowed hard and rested her head against his chest for a moment. She loved him so much and wished she could tell him so. "Max . . . you are such a dear man. When I first started dreaming about you, I knew you were a hero."

He tilted her face up and kissed her mouth with unerring aim even in the blackness that surrounded them like a heavy blanket. "And when was it that you started dreaming about me, Ms. Leslie?"

"Long before I met you," she said, and embarked on the story of how he had come into her dreams when her sister had told her that she wanted a new husband, a father for her children. "I conjured you up for Sharon, or maybe my Gypsy multiple-great-grandmother did, and ran those ads for my sister's sake. But when you appeared long after I'd come to the conclusion that I was out of my skull for even thinking about finding a mate for her that way, I knew I wanted you for myself."

"You've got me, sweet. All you have to do is reach out and take me."

Instead, she shifted away from him, turned on his flashlight, and slowly led the way back to the rock fall.

* * *

"Jeanie . . ." She knew by the soft gentleness of his tone that Max was about to impart bad news. She turned from rolling a rock into the ever-enlarging pile she'd been building now for two and a half long days. At least she thought that was how long it had been. Max's watch had been smashed when a rock had rolled over it. His face, in the dim glow cast by his dying flashlight, was pale under the dirt and lined with exhaustion. His eyes, usually so intense a blue that she could focus on them and believe she was seeing sky again, were dull with defeat.

"There's a rock here, honey. It must be a slab from the ceiling. I can't dig my way around it. I've been trying for hours. The only way through it would be with blasting powder or a rock drill, and I'm fresh out of both. I'm sorry, Jeanie. I tried."

She crawled to him, and, for the first time, turned off the flashlight voluntarily. In the dark, she held him. "I know you did, Max. I know. Oh, you tried so hard. No one could have done more than you. But don't forget. There's the other passage we haven't worked on yet. You rest. I'll get started on it. It's only little stuff. I can move it by myself." She felt him shake his head in protest and gave him a hard squeeze.

"This time, McKenzie, *you* are going to do what *I* tell you! Got it?"

"Yes, ma'am," he said, chuckling, and she felt better at once. By now they knew the cave well enough to crawl to the higher part without the light. She got him settled on a shelf above the creek, then pulled the sleeping bag out of her way, turned on the light briefly to place their food supplies in a safer location, and washed her hands. Her gloves had long since been tattered beyond being any use. That done, she fetched both of them drinks of water and small handfuls of almonds.

After a brief stop to drink and munch the nuts, she began a careful excavation of the second rock fall, finding it just as slow going as Max had the first. For each rock she pulled out, three more rolled down to take its place. For each handful of rubble she scooped onto Max's slicker, which they had been using as a sled for the smaller stuff, more slid in, but she kept on. When Max insisted on spelling her, she continued to work, hauling the debris out of the way. Then it was her turn again to work in the cramped confines of the tiny hole they were digging.

When her hand poked through and met nothing but air on the other side, at first she didn't recognize the significance of what had happened. But when she saw a faint glimmer of pale, washed-out light, she let out a cry so full of hoarse triumph that Max whirled around and staggered to where she crouched.

"Look!" she cried, backing out to let him in. "We're through! I can see light out there, Max! Oh, Lord, dig, Max! Dig!"

He didn't need her encouragement, but scrabbled at the rock, lifting out one crumbling piece after another, rolling them down toward her where she caught them and tumbled them anywhere; it no longer mattered, in minutes they'd be free! When the hole was large enough for him to fit his head and shoulders through, he squirmed in, and she heard him groan.

"It's just another cave," he said, worming his

way back out to where she crouched, her face alight with hope. "As far as I can see, it's a little bigger around then this, but with no side passages leading anywhere."

The hope refused to die in her eyes. "But the light?" she demanded. "Max, I could see light!"

"Yes, honey, I know. There's a small hole in the roof." He rubbed a hand over the long stubble on his face, then looked at her again as he slumped against the rough wall, exhausted and disheartened. "But the roof is at least forty feet overhead."

Nine

It was a disaster, but somehow less of a disaster than the immovable slab that blocked the way to the outside. At least, to Jeanie's relief, her feelings of claustrophobia lessened when she could see that tiny, unreachable slit of daylight, even now beginning to fade as yet another night fell.

They moved their equipment into the larger cavern, finding a wider, more level ledge there for their sleeping bag, and another where they stored their dwindling supply of food. The stream that trickled through was larger in the other cave, with a deeper pool. And just before the water disappeared into a subterranean crack, there was an outcrop that permitted Jeanie to feel more private straddling the stream to take care of the call of nature.

Standing with their heads back, facing the tiny slit of sky overhead, they took turns shouting, but no one responded, no face appeared to block the light.

"I'm going to have a bath," Jeanie said, fighting

despair. "I'm dirty and I smell bad and I am not going to spend one more night like this."

"Jeanie, you'll freeze! That water's cold."

"I'll be quick, but I'm going to do it. Go sit on the other side of the cave and don't watch me."

"I'd like nothing better than to watch you have a bath," he said, "well, almost nothing; a hot fudge sundae would beat even that. But how can I watch you? It's dark in here, in case you hadn't noticed."

"I mean, don't turn the light on me."

"I promise, not unless it sounds as if the sharks have you by the feet."

He was right. It was frigid water, but when she was out and rubbing herself with her extra T-shirt, she knew it had been worth it. "Max," she said excitedly, zipping up her jeans as she stumbled to where he sat. He turned the flash on briefly to light her way. "We can build a fire! I saw matches in your pack. It'll help keep us warm, and the smoke coming out of the ground will tell someone we're here!"

He pulled her down beside him on the sleeping bag. "I don't think five comic books will make much smoke, Jeanie. Even if we added our backpacks and all our clothes and could get them to burn, this is a good-size cavern and it would take an awful lot of smoke to fill it enough and get it going out that little-bitty hole way up there.

"Max, you're not thinking! Where are we?"

He stared at her before he flicked off the light. "In a cave."

"What kind of a cave? Why are we both so dirty all the time? What turns our hands and faces so black, we look like Vaudeville performers? What about all those rocks we've been moving? Max, they are coal! Coal burns! We can build a fire with coal, make lots of dirty, black smoke. Surely, surely, it will be seen!"

He stared at her. "Jeanie, honey, you're the one not thinking. Where is the draft coming from?" He looked up at where the slit of daylight had once been visible. "Up there, right? And that's the only place it's coming from. If we lit a coal fire, the fumes and gases would be driven down into the cave, and they'd kill us as surely as if the entire roof collapsed on us. That's just one of the many ways coal miners used to die—from gases in the mines if a fire started. I'm sorry to burst your bubble, but remember, with that little hole up there, and people out looking for us, we have a better chance of being found tomorrow than we ever had today. Tomorrow, we can holler ourselves hoarse, but not if we're dead from coal gases."

"You're right, I guess." She swallowed her disappointment. But she wasn't quite ready to give up. "Max . . . heat rises. Maybe if our fire was hot enough, the gases would go out too. Are you sure about the danger of gases?"

He hesitated. "Not absolutely. But sure enough that I'm not willing to risk it. If there was another source of air coming in, or a place for what's coming in to go out, then I'd go for it like a shot. But I don't think there is."

"But there must be a place for it to go out. Otherwise, there wouldn't be a draft."

He sighed. "You're right about that, of course, but it's not a very big draft. And don't forget, there's probably just impenetrable forest up there. Even if it was safe for us to make smoke signals, nobody would see them."

This time, she sighed. She knew he was right on all counts. The risks far outweighed any possible benefits to building a coal fire. She briefly considered that they start piling rocks in the middle of the cave to get to a point high enough to reach out, but recognized that as another desperate act, perfectly useless. So was damming the stream's outlet and floating up as the cave filled. Clearly, she'd read too many comic books as a child. She patted Jason's little pile. Lord, but she hoped he was curled up safely at home reading comic books. But if he was, why hadn't he told anybody about his cave? Why hadn't he suggested that his aunt might have found it and been lost inside it? What if he had and no one believed him? What if . . . There were too many what-ifs. She shivered and pulled her down jacket more tightly around her.

Max turned on the light and got to his feet. "And now, since you're so clean and pink and not suffering visibly from hypothermia, I think I'm going to avail myself of your bathtub too."

She looked down at her hands. "Don't you mean clean and sort of dingy gray?"

"Whatever," he said. "It's good enough for me."

That night, as they lay on the sleeping bag under the blanket, Max thought he heard Jeanie weeping softly.

He held her, as he had every night they had spent in the cave, and said, "Are you crying, sweetheart?"

"No. Of course not. Well, maybe just a little." Her laugh was uncertain. "Funny, I don't remember the last time I really cried."

"Why is that?"

"Why? I don't know. Lousy memory, I guess."

"Dope." His tone and the hand that stroked her hair were both tender. "I meant, why do you cry so seldom that you can't recall the last time? I thought tears were considered a legitimate female release."

She smiled in the dark, remembering all of a sudden that it hadn't been so long ago that she'd cried for that kind of release. It had been the night he'd walked out on her after reading aloud that sexy letter he'd been writing. Then, she'd cried from disappointment, frustration, and rage. Or so she'd told herself.

"For release of tension, I run. What do you do?"

"Pummel a punching bag."

There was a long silence before he said, "What would you most like to see right now, besides the outside of this cave."

"Daffodils," she replied without hesitation. "A field full of daffodils all bright and yellow with the sun shining down on them. Green spears of leaves, the first drowsy bumblebees of the year coating their legs with golden pollen. I love daffodils so much. They are so bright and lively and have such a delicate scent. I wish, just once more, I could see and smell a daffodil."

He wished that, just once, he could give her a hundred dozen daffodils. He said nothing, only held her tighter.

"I wonder why they haven't found the rockfall from the outside yet?"

He had to tell her now about the tape he hadn't had to tie to the cedar bough. After a long silence during which she simply clung to him, she asked, "We're going to die in here, aren't we, Max?"

He longed to be able to lie to her about that too. "I think we could, honey." Searches, he knew, couldn't be kept up forever. The cost in time and manpower was too great. He only hoped, for her poor sister's sake, that she hadn't lost her son permanently as well. Jeanie rarely mentioned Jason now, but on the occasions when she did, it was with such certainty of his safety that he was touched by her faith. He wondered why she didn't have that same blind faith in her own invincibility.

"I'm so sorry I got you into this. If it hadn't been for me, you'd never have been here."

"If I have to die, Jeanie, don't you realize I'd rather do it with you in my arms than anyone else?"

She lifted herself up on an elbow and found his face with her hand. His beard was growing soft now, and she liked to stroke it. "Max? Will you make love with me? I don't want to die never having known what it's like to love you."

He didn't reply, just reached up and slowly slid the blanket back. Just as slowly, he found the tab of the zipper on her jacket and pulled it down, then laid her on her back. His hand softly encircled her throat, and he cradled her chin. Tilting her face up to his, their mouths came together sweetly, seekingly, lovingly.

"I don't know if I can, sweetheart," he said softly, "but I sure want to give it a try."

When his hand slid under her sweatshirt, moved gently over her bony rib cage and covered a breast that had been much fuller five—or was it six?—days before, Max wanted to weep for the losses they had both sustained. If he had been a praying man, he'd have prayed for the strength to give her all the power of the physical love he had wanted to share with her for so long. But now he wasn't certain he could do more than caress her, pleasure her with his hands and mouth. She sighed, and he knew he was succeeding at least in part.

"Be careful," she whispered. "Your poor hands are so sore."

"Never too sore to touch you," he murmured against the soft skin of her neck, "never could I pass up an opportunity to give you pleasure. But if they're too rough for you, I'll just love you with my mouth."

Her breath caught in her throat. "With everything, Max. Everything you can. I want all of you in every way."

It broke his heart, but he had to warn her. "Sweetheart, I'm weak. I may not be able to—"

She stopped him with her mouth over his, a long, deep kiss that made him wonder if overexertion and lack of food for five days would cause the problems he anticipated. "Max, my darling, I know that and I don't care! Just being with you like this, holding you, kissing you, hearing your voice is enough. There are many ways of making love, and what we're doing is just one of them. Tell me . . . talk to me the way you did in those letters you wrote. They drove me so crazy with wanting you, I nearly died."

"Writing them was almost as sweet a torture as knowing what they were doing to you." She felt the warmth of his soft laughter against her chest and rejoiced that they could still have fun together, even though it might be all they'd ever have.

He began to speak as he had written, telling her all the things he planned to do to her, everything he wanted her to do to him, the way he would make her feel, the sensations her touches would arouse in him, did arouse in him, were arousing in him.

"Max!" she gasped as her nipple peaked hard into his palm. He found the other with his lips, sucked on it, and was delighted by her moan of pleasure. She said his name in that soft, husky, sexy voice that had been one of the first things about her to attract him. Strength he'd thought long since played out with escape attempts came flooding back, and he hardened within the confines of his jeans. She moved her hips against his, and he knew she felt it, exulted in it as much as he did. She parted the front of his jacket, slipped her hands under his sweater, and ran her fingers into the hair on his chest, finding his nipples and teasing them as he teased hers.

"Max . . . please, no clothes between us." Her voice was ragged, urgent.

"Sweetheart, I don't want you to be cold," he protested, but she was shrugging out of her jacket, peeling her sweatshirt off over her head, and even in the utter darkness, he knew exactly how lovely she must look. He felt her slither out of her jeans, and then he capitulated, stripping himself as swiftly as she had. When their naked bodies came together, there was no more thought of cold or worries of impotence. Heat grew, spread, sparked between them. Hands explored rigid flesh, soft, moist hollows. Tongues entwined, limbs tangled, bodies strained, and two voices called out low as he lunged inside her, unable to wait, to prolong the foreplay. Her silken thighs wrapped tightly around his hips as she accepted him gladly with a little cry of welcome, drawing him deep within.

"Ah, Jeanie, baby, beautiful!" He pulled almost

out and then eased back into her with tantalizing slowness that forced her to thrust her hips up to him, wordlessly begging for more. Once again, he withdrew, paused, then slowly, inch by teasing inch, reinserted himself within her pulsating folds, feeling her quivering anticipation of the moment when they would be fully joined again. It was as he had known it would be, exquisite torture for them both, and he never wanted it to stop. But she had other ideas, more urgent needs, if that were possible, and she dug her fingers hard into his taut buttocks, rocking hard up against him.

"Max! Max! Don't stop now! I need you so much!"

He called out her name, driving into her again and again, feeling her legs tighten around him, her fingers dig into his back, her whole body arch into a taut bow reaching for that one, seemingly impossible goal.

High-pitched, keening wails emanated from her. Her muscles tightened around him, triggering his own climax. It came with a rush, draining him, until he collapsed atop her, as her spasms subsided too. Like hers, his breath sobbed in and out, but he was more satisfied than he had ever been in his entire life. And more spent.

Sometime later he realized they were both shivering in the cold. Waking her gently, he tugged her down jacket around her, pulled his own back on, and drew the blanket over their bodies again. Their own heat was trapped there, and they slept again, exhausted. But as daylight sent its one little finger into the crack high overhead, they awoke, opened their eyes, and smiled at each other, their eyes full of joyous memories of what they had discovered together deep inside the cave that might well become their tomb.

Beside them, the little stream played its tinkling morning music that sounded strangely to Jeanie like the jingling of golden bangles, and she was happy.

Every night after their day's attempts at freeing themselves, they lay still and listened in vain for the sound of voices, the sound of traffic, even the dull rumble of a passing jet to let them know that others humans still lived on the surface of the earth they were trapped within. But all they heard was the gentle, musical tune of the busy little stream as it came from one seam in the rock, crossed their cavern, and slipped away into another small crack.

But still, the musical creek was a pleasant melody to fall asleep to, and exhaustion kept them from staying awake too long brooding.

"There are twenty-eight mints left," Jeanie said, looking up from the ledge where she knelt, "a handful of raisins and six dried apricots. What would you like for dinner?"

"One apricot, six raisins, and a mint."

"Sounds good to me too," she said, carrying him his share, making sure he got the larger of the two apricots. Carefully, she fed him. His hands were too swollen and torn for him to do much for himself. Since they had entered the larger cave, and all of their shouting had shown no results, they had gone back into the first cavern and tried again and again in the dark to dislodge that immovable slab.

They had taken apart the two backpacks, straightened the aluminum frames as best they could and tied them together with pieces of cloth. But even with Jeanie standing on Max's shoulders, their rod was a good twenty or thirty feet short of reaching the slit in the roof. As each night fell, they bathed together in the pool, dried each other, and then cuddled together on Jason's sleeping bag, covered with their coats and the blanket.

Whenever their strength permitted it, they awoke, stroked each other, nibbled a few bites of their remaining supplies, and sometimes, but not always, made love. Often it was simply enough to lie together, naked under the blanket and touch, talk, whisper secrets no one else would ever know, of hopes and dreams and memories.

Their strength was waning daily, and they both knew it, but whenever they awoke and there was light coming in from the other world, there was a moment to rejoice in another day of life, another day when they might be found. At night, they knew there was no possibility of discovery, so the dark hours were theirs, and in them they shared a gentle, weary kind of loving.

"Good morning," he said, on what Jeanie thought was the beginning of their sixth day in the larger cavern.

"Good morning," she responded. *Good morning, my love*, she added silently, wondering if he could read the words in her eyes.

"Did you sleep well?"

"I had the craziest dream about a blue-eyed hero." she told him. "It seems he undressed me, made the most exquisite love to me, and then held me in his arms all night long."

"That's funny," he said. "I had a similar dream. But in mine, the most beautiful woman sat up beside me in the dark and took off all her clothes, then attacked me. I fought, of course, but she's a witch and was able to overcome my objections with no difficulty."

She laughed softly. "Maybe, in spite of not being the dark-haired sister, she's a Gypsy after all."

"Uh-uh." He shook his head. "She's a witch, because I've been totally bewitched ever since she first came into my dreams."

That she could relate to. She brushed her mouth over his. "I've heard that dreams can be prophetic. I wonder if something like either of our dreams is ever going to happen?"

"I don't know," he said, "but I kind of like yours. Want to give it a try?"

It worked with no trouble at all.

They both knew now, and were ready to admit to each other as well as themselves, that escape attempts were futile. If they were going to die slowly and lingeringly as their food ran out, it was better to conserve their strength for the joy they could give each other rather than waste it in more exhausting and useless digging. If they were to have nothing else in this life, then at least they could have each other.

Sometimes when they were awake, there was daylight coming through the tiny slit. Sometimes, it was very black. But once, just once, a bright, full moon cast a romantic glow against one wall.

"I want to make love to you in the moonlight," Max said, forcing her to bestir herself. He gave her a mint to suck and carried their bed and clothing to the far side of the cave, where the faint, ghostly glow shone. Placing the sleeping bag in its beam, he came back for her and led her there, laid her down and knelt before her. Bending, he pressed his mouth over hers. When she moaned softly and lifted herself slightly toward him, he took one nipple in his mouth, then moved to the other until they both stood high and shiny and wet, glistening in the moonbeam.

"Love me," she whispered. "Come inside me and love me just once more."

"Can't, sweetheart," he said, knowing it was true. He was growing too weak. He rested his head on her warm stomach, caressing her with his hand, parting her thighs and finding the moist folds between, then kissing her there.

She had about as much strength as he had and could only sigh softly as the gentle pleasure began to curl within her. Her knees lifted and fell apart. She cradled his head in her hands while he kissed her intimately. Her climax was small and weak, but no less beautiful, because he had given it to her. Drawing him into her arms, holding his head against her breasts, she whispered to him, "Max McKenzie, I have a confession to make. I love you. With all my heart and soul, I love you."

"Ahh, darling. Then if we were going to live, you'd marry me?"

She hesitated only briefly. What harm could it do now to make him as happy as he had just made her? "Yes, Max. I'd marry you."

She felt his smile against her breasts. Moments passed. The moonbeam moved away from their tiny share of the sky, and it was dark again. She thought he slept, but then he began to hum. *I do . . . love you . . . with all my heart . . . The Hawaiian Wedding Song?*

Her heart swelled. Was he saying he loved her? "Max? Max, what are you humming?"

"Don't know," he muttered. "Just humming along."

"With what?"

"The harmonica."

Harmonica? Was he hallucinating? She listened, but all she could hear was the babble of the stream and . . . wait! No, it couldn't be! She shoved him off her and sat up. There it was, the sound of a harmonica being played somewhere up there in the night.

Leaping to her feet, she screamed with all her might, "Help! Help! We're down here! Help!"

"Who's there? Who are you?" The voice was faint and seemed to be fading even as the man called.

"We're underground!" Max projected his voice as hard as he could. "We're in a cave. There's a hole in the roof. Be careful!"

There was no reply. Jeanie waited and waited, then tipped back her head and screamed for all she was worth. "Help! We're here!"

"I hear you!" came the voice again, this time more clearly. "But where are you?"

"We're buried in a cave!" Max tried once more, but again there was no reply.

"It's my voice he can hear," Jeanie cried. "It's higher pitched. It carries better." She moved to the area just beneath the hole and screamed again. "Help!"

"Listen to me!" The man's voice was fainter.

"I can't find you now. It's too dark. Stay right where you are. I'm tying my shirt to a tree so I won't lose the place where I first heard you. I'm going for help. I will be back. I promise. Call, lady, if you can hear me."

Jeanie screamed a yes. Her throat ached and burned, but she screamed as if her life depended on it. And it did.

"Okay!" came the man's voice. "Are you Jeanie Leslie?"

"Yes!" she shouted, her voice cracking.

"Is Max McKenzie with you?"

Again she gave a loud affirmative.

"Are either of you hurt?"

"No! No! We are all right! Jason! Is Jason safe?"

"Yes! The boy is fine! I'm leaving now, but I'm coming back. Don't go away!"

Jeanie collapsed, laughing and crying, onto the hard floor of the cave. "He's okay, Max! Jason is all right! Did you hear the man? He said Jason's fine!"

Max, crouching naked over her, tried to lift her to her feet but could not. Trembling, so weak he could barely stand, he brought their bed to where she was and rolled her onto it, holding her tightly until they slept.

Pieces of rock falling around her roused Jeanie in the morning. Their chink of daylight was slightly larger, and suddenly she realized they were both stark naked. "Can you hear me?" asked a voice, not, she thought, the one from the night before. "Is anyone down there?"

"Yes!" she cried hoarsely, her throat still sore from screaming the previous night. "We're here. We are right under you. Stop throwing rocks!"

"Okay, Jeanie, you and Max move aside. We have to make this hole big enough to get someone down to you. Get way over to the wall where it's safest. Can you both move?"

"Yes!" She could, but she wasn't so certain about Max. He was lying inert on the sleeping bag, staring at her as if wondering who she might be talking to.

She shook him to get his attention. "Max!" she said urgently, "come on. Get with it. We have to get dressed. Help is coming. Here, let me get you up." With difficulty, she led him to a safer area, then went back and got their bedding and clothes. "Can you get into your jeans?" she asked. He nodded. She handed them to him and tugged on her own, amazed at how loosely they fit. She pulled on her filthy sweatshirt, her damp gray socks, and her less-wet sneakers, while Max forced his shaggy head through the neck of his grimy, matted wool sweater. In the meantime, more chunks of rock fell down around where they had been sleeping, and then the light was blocked and a man in jeans and a bright orange jacket came through the hole, lowered on a cable.

Unhooking himself, he ran to them. Kneeling beside them, he reached out to touch Max. "Damn!" he said, his voice choking, moisture filling his green eyes. "The things you won't do for a good story, Max. And who is this? The coal miner's daughter?"

Max lifted his blackened hand, touched his brother's golden hair, said, "Hi, Rolph. Nope, this is no coal miner's daughter. This is my personal chunk of coal. Squeeze coal, and what do you get? Diamonds." He let his hand fall from Rolph's hair to Jeanie's lap. "I squeezed her. Believe me, she's a diamond." He smiled just before he passed out cold across Jeanie's thighs.

Ten

Two paramedics followed Rolph down the cable next, bringing flasks of hot beef broth with them. "Slowly," said one man to Jeanie, when she started to gulp the wonderful liquid. "Nice and easy. One sip at a time." More rescuers arrived, Max came to and sat up, leaning half against the wall, half against Jeanie.

The cavern was flooded with light, stretchers were prepared, and as she leaned on Max and he on her, sipping their broth, the hole became even wider at the top.

"Jason? Please tell me about my nephew!"

She asked again. She'd been asking, but the crew had been too busy looking after her and Mac to give her any details other than to say he was fine.

Now, as she was lifted, carried away from Max's comforting warmth and laid on a stretcher, one of the paramedics told her that her nephew had been found early the second day of search. He'd fallen into a ravine and had been suffering from a gash to the head, a severe concussion, a broken leg, and a badly bruised shoulder. He was recovering at home after a stay in hospital, and now that she had been found, he'd recover a lot faster.

"How long were we in here?" she asked, and was amazed at the answer.

"Ten days? I had it somewhere around seven, maybe eight at the most. Listen, get Max out first. He's weaker than I am. He worked a lot harder. Please, take care of him." She burst into tears she could not seem to control.

"My partner's taking care of him just fine, Jeanie. Now don't you worry." The paramedic pulled her arm free of her jacket, shoved up the sleeve of her sweatshirt, and swabbed a place clean on her skin, before popping a needle in. "You afraid of heights?" he asked.

"No, just caves," she said wearily. "I'm so tired. I want to go home."

He smiled and patted her grimy cheek. "Then up you go, sweetie. You're on your way home. I promise Max will be right behind you." He spoke into a hand-held radio and steadied her cradlelike stretcher as it was hoisted aloft. Soon she was in the daylight, blessed rain falling on her face, and Sharon was rushing along beside her, as she was carried at a trot through the woods. Sharon's cold fingers clung to Jeanie's wrist, avoiding her swollen, bleeding hand with its jagged nails and torn skin. Every so often, she'd reach out and stroke the dirty, tangled hair back from her sister's face, smearing the endless tears that fell.

"Oh, baby, baby, I thought you were dead!"

"Who, me?" Jeanie tried to smile but couldn't. Her mouth twisted, and she cried along with her sister. "Who'd look after you if I let myself spend the rest of my life in a cave?"

Sharon paled slightly, and Jeanie knew it had been tactless joke; she had come too close to doing just that to try to make light of it. "What's this for?" she complained when she was being lifted into the back of a waiting ambulance, struggling against the restraints that held her in the stretcher. "I don't need an ambulance. I just want to go home!"

"You're going to the hospital for a checkup." There was a no-nonsense quality in the older sister's tone as Sharon climbed in beside her, the doors were slammed, and the vehicle started moving.

"No! Wait! Max!" She had to fight against a heavy feeling of sleepiness to get the words out.

"Max is coming right behind us, babe," Sharon said soothingly. "His brother is with him, and his parents are waiting at the hospital. We've all been frantic, Jeanie. This has been the most terrible period in my entire life, almost as bad as it must have been for you. Now shut up, close your eyes, and just let me look at you so I can convince myself you're really here."

Jeanie wanted to tell her sister that in some ways it had also been the most wonderful period in her life, but not even Sharon could be expected to understand the special magic of what she and Max had discovered as they lay together entombed in a coal mine. She closed her eyes, and when she opened them again, she was lying in a warm bed and a uniformed nurse was carefully working up a gray-colored lather on her right arm. That hand and the left as well, were already clean and pink and swathed in bandages.

"Max?" she whispered.

"On the second floor, men's medical," said the nurse, smiling. "You've got to be the grubbiest patient I've ever had, Ms. Leslie. You look like a coal miner."

Jeanie made herself laugh, but it wasn't easy.

"When can I see . . ." she had been going to say Max, but realized maybe patients weren't allowed to see each other in hospitals, so she changed it, and said weakly, ". . . my nephew?"

"As soon as you're clean enough for him to recognize you, I promise to wheel him in here personally. He was released a few days ago, and his mother is on her way home right now to get him. He wants to see you too."

"I don't know why I have to be here." Suddenly her eyes filled with tears, and she was crying again, sobbing as if she would never be able to stop. "I'm not sick and I want to go home and I want to see Max right now!"

"I know, I know." The nurse's voice was soothing. "But you're badly malnourished, and it's best if you stay here for a little while to get built back up." She wiped Jeanie's tears with a tissue and continued with the bed bath, removing all traces of grime from her skin. "Look, now. You're right beside the biggest window we could find. Your Max insisted that we put you beside a window before he'd let us do anything to him. I promise you'll get to see him soon, too, if you just cooperate and give me your other arm. You wouldn't want him to see you looking like this, would you?"

Jeanie didn't bother to tell the nurse that Max had seen her looking a heck of a lot worse in the past few days and had made slow and wonderful love with her in spite of that.

"Promise me one more thing," she bargained.

"Sure. What's that?"

"Get him a hot fudge sundae. He really, really wants one."

"I'll see to it that the staff on his floor knows about that just as soon as I'm done with you. You two must really love each other a whole lot, huh? He wants you to have a window, and you want him to have a sundae. Those were the things each of you missed the most?"

Jeanie nodded. "Something like that." She sniffed and wiped her eyes on one shoulder of her pale yellow hospital gown. "I want a shower. I need to wash my hair." Her eyes continued to leak helpless tears.

"Tomorrow you can have a soak in the bath, if you promise to keep your bandages out of the water. In about ten minutes, someone is going to come in and give you a shampoo, so don't worry about that."

Jeanie's tears stopped. "A shampoo?"

"In a proper, portable shampoo chair with a basin attached. We're swiping it from the extended care unit just for you."

"A real, honest-to-goodness shampoo?"

The nurse nodded. "You got it, kiddo."

Jeanie was as amazed as the aide who scrubbed her head at the amount of grime that came out of it, at the number of lathers and rinses it took to make her hair clean again. She didn't care even one iota that her hair was being left to dry naturally into a zillion ditzy kinks that made her look like a brunette Little Orphan Annie. It was enough to be clean all over. When she was helped back into her bed, she was so weak and weary that she no longer objected to a brief hospital stay. She slept until someone brought her a bowl of banana custard and an orange, plus a little paper cupful of vitamins and a milkshake. She downed all of it but the last half of the shake.

And then, the first nurse came back, wheeling Jason, followed by Sharon.

"I'm sorry I got lost and got you lost too," said Jason. "I fell down a steep cliff and got hurt. I was going to visit my friend, but I saw a brown rabbit and chased it, then I fell."

Sharon's mouth tightened, but she said nothing as Jeanie leaned out of her bed to hug her nephew gently, mindful of his bruised shoulder. "Honey, I'm just glad you're safe, and that we found your cave. If it hadn't been for your sleeping bag and beans and cookies, Max and I would be in a lot worse shape than we are now." She looked pleadingly at her sister. "Can you get in to see him? I have to know how he is! They aren't telling me a thing."

"I saw Zinnie in the elevator. She say's he's doing fine. Like you, he was being cleaned up and fed."

"Zinnie?"

"Max's mother. Short for Zinnia. She and her husband, Harry, and Max's brother, Rolph, have been staying with me while the search went on." She smiled. "They're wonderful people, Jeanie. So strong and supportive of each other and of me and the kids. Having them with me made the days so much easier to bear for all of us. By the way, Roxy sends her love. She wanted to come, but I promised her you'd be there tomorrow when she gets home from school."

"Oh, I can't wait to get home!" Jeanie felt her chin wobble and steadied it with difficulty. "We thought the search must have been called off," she said, a shudder shaking her skinny frame. "It was so long, so very long, and we couldn't expect people to keep risking their own lives for us. But I don't understand why they didn't find Jason's cave, or at least where it had collapsed."

Jason looked mystified. "Aunt Jeanie, I don't have a cave."

She stared at him. "What? But Jase, we followed a trail that ended at a big cedar tree. I looked under the low branches, hoping you'd be there, and saw another trail. And then I saw a little slot in the cliff. I shined my light in and saw a bit of red. I thought it was your ski jacket, so I went in after you."

Sharon's eyes widened. "You went into that cave voluntarily? Jeanie, you're afraid of small places! You won't even use elevators! Why in the world would you go into a cave?"

"For Jason! I saw something red. I thought it was him. I had to. Don't you see? I had to do it, only it wasn't his jacket, it was his sleeping bag." She leaned back wearily on her pillows. "I thought it was his, anyway. It looked like the one I bought him last year for his birthday. But I guess any red sleeping bag is the same as any other."

"My sleeping bag's at home, Aunt Jeanie. I don't go into caves. You and Mom have told me often enough how dangerous they can be."

"Some child planned on spending the night in that cave," Jeanie said. "He had left his sleeping bag, a can of beans, a stack of comics, and a bag of cookies." She bit her lip, a look of consternation crossing her face, but Sharon allayed her new fear at once.

"There are no other people missing." She smiled. "No people missing at all, now that you and Max have been found."

Sharon touched her sister's face with a gentle hand, her joy shining clearly out of her jet black eyes. "But imagine you diving into a cave, Jeanie! It boggles the mind. I thought you and Max had fallen in through the hole at the top! Everyone thinks that! The doctors are all saying what a miracle it is you don't both have multiple fractures and the PEP people are ready to string Max up for not tying markers to the area you were searching!"

"It wasn't Max's fault! None of it was. He was fantastic, Sharon. He tried and tried to dig us out. We shouted and shouted. Then, last night, we heard the harmonica man. Who is he, Sharon? I want to meet him, to thank him for being out there in the woods in the moonlight playing his harmonica. He was playing *The Hawaiian Wedding Song.*"

Sharon didn't answer. Jason did. With a defiant look on his face he said, "His name is Marc Duval. He's my friend. I wanted to see him the night I lied and told Mom I was going to Mark's—the other Mark's. He's neat, Aunt Jeanie. You'd like him. So would Mom, if she'd just meet him."

"Jason," Sharon said, her face set into stubborn lines, "we won't discuss it right now."

"But, Mom—"

"Jason. We do not know Mr. Duval. He is not your friend. He is an acquaintance you made without my knowledge, and I don't consider him a proper friend for a little boy. Now, I know you've been lost and injured and worried about your auntie Jeanie, but that doesn't mean you can get away with disobeying me. You are not to have anything more to do with Mr. Duval. We are all very grateful to him for being where he was when he was, and finding Aunt Jeanie and Max, but that is as far as it goes. Do you understand?"

Jason drew in a long breath, and Jeanie, her eyes darting from mother to son, fully expected a rebellious tirade. But her nephew nodded. "Yeah. Okay, sure, Mom," he said, then he blurted out to his aunt, "He makes music all the time, just like Mom used to do. I like to hear him. I miss the music."

Jeanie saw Sharon's face turn white and pain flood her jet eyes, but before she could mediate the brewing battle, there was a commotion in the hallway that distracted them. She heard a man say, "She may be sleeping. Just let me check," but the door was thrust open without ceremony, and Max strode through, pushing an I.V. pole before him. His eyes went at once to Jeanie's face. His own closed for a second, and he swayed on his feet, reached out to clumsily balance himself on the back of Sharon's chair.

Sitting down, apparently not minding that anyone else was present, Max gathered Jeanie into his arms and held her. "Oh, Lord," he said softly, his face buried in her damp mass of curly hair. "Oh, Lord. Oh, Lord. Oh, Lord."

When Jeanie looked up moments later, they were alone in the room.

He was clean, but still wore his short, dark beard. His eyes shone like bright blue lights from under his brows. "Are you all right?" She gently touched the point where the I.V. needle went into his skin.

"I'm fine. That's just for some antibiotics, they tell me. My fingers are infected. Are you okay?"

"I'm fine. A little pudding, an orange, and half a tiny milk shake filled me to the brim. Have you been eating?"

His smile deepened. "Two hot fudge sundaes. I'm told I have you to thank for that."

She stroked his fuzzy face with her bandaged hand, wishing she could feel it with her palm. She settled for rubbing her cheek against it. "And thank you for my window. Max, it's all over, isn't it? We aren't dreaming this?"

"We aren't dreaming, Jeanie, but no, it's not all over. It's only beginning." Holding her hair down at the sides of her head, he kissed her. "When, sweetheart? When can we get married?"

She was silent for a long moment, staring at him in utter dismay. "Married?" She echoed his word in a troubled whisper. "Max, we can't. I can't. No. Please I . . ."

"But you said it!" he protested. "In the cave you said you would marry me if we were going to live, and, Jeanie, we are!"

"But . . . not together." Tears filled her eyes, and she blinked them back. She had cried enough to last for the rest of her life.

"Ahh, Jeanie, you said you would. You did. I wasn't dreaming that. I want you, Jeanie. I need you. Don't turn me away. Remember, you dreamed me up first." He tried to smile, tried to joke, but his blue eyes were filled with nothing but pain. "I'm your hero, remember? How can you possibly turn down a hero?"

"I said if we were going to live, I'd want to marry

you. But then I thought we were going to die. I said it to give you something, Max, to comfort you, to ease your suffering if only a little, to give back to you some of the pleasure you'd given me."

"You said you loved me."

She swallowed the hard, high lump in her throat and met his gaze. "I do," she said softly. "I'm sorry. I know you hate it when women do that, but it's not something I can help."

"I don't find myself hating it when you say it."

"But you can't say it back to me, can you?"

Misery made his shoulders droop. He let his hands fall and slipped from the side of her bed to the chair Sharon had used. "I would, Jeanie. If I could. If I knew what it meant, if I wasn't sure it was just words, then I'd give them to you the way you gave me your promise of marriage. But if I did, it would mean exactly what your words meant: comfort, ease, an attempt to give you back some of the pleasures you've given me.

"If you love me, if you've figured out what it means, and if it's something so big and so wonderful that it can go on forever, then why not marry me and have forever? It's what I'm offering you."

"No. What you're offering me isn't enough. And I truly don't want marriage. Max, my freedom is so important to me, I don't think I'll ever be able to make you understand. When we were in that cave, all I wanted was out. I think if I were locked into marriage, I'd feel the same. And I don't want to do that to you. I'd fight against you and our marriage, the boundaries it would erect around me as hard as I fought against the walls of that cavern."

"I would let you be free, Jeanie. I wouldn't try

to stop you from being you. We are free, free of that cave, free of whatever barriers society might expect us to erect around each other. We can do whatever we want, make our own rules within the unit our marriage would make."

She was silent for several minutes, then looked out the wide window at her side. There was a world out there. It was open and it was hers, and she knew she had to walk through it without anyone to hold her back, build her fences—make dark closets. Slowly, she shook her head. "I'm sorry, Max. So sorry."

He got to his feet, one hand wrapped around the pole for support.

"I'm sorry, too, Jeanie. Sorry for you. Because whether you know it or not, you're still locked up in your grandfather's basement closet, and I don't think you'll ever find a way out. You're still trapped, but I'm free. Free to get over wanting you," he added bitterly. "And I will."

"Good. There are plenty of women out there willing to help you. And I'll get over loving you."

"Maybe so," he said, his blue eyes somber on her face. "But you'll never get over being a coward, Jeanie. And whether you like it or not, you're still trapped in a cave of your own making. A cave of fear. It's ironic, isn't it, that the trap you fear the most is the one that holds you the tightest?"

"It's just as ironic that the love you despise so much is the one thing women want most to give you. And yet you won't give it in return because you fear looking like a fool. Well, you may never look like one, my beautiful, blue-eyed hero, but you are one, Max. The biggest fool of them all."

He turned on his heel and walked away, green hospital bathrobe flapping at the backs of his hairy legs, silly paper slippers scuffing along the floor. As the door closed, Jeanie's eyes closed, but even that didn't stop the stupid, helpless tears from escaping again.

The next morning, they let her go.

"Jeanie, you're going to have to eat something. If anything, you've lost weight since you came out of hospital. And when are you going back to work?"

"Tired of me, Sharon?"

"As a matter of fact, yes! I'm tired of you dragging around here looking like a wraith. So you had a fight with Max. Don't you think it's time you made it up? Emotions were bound to be running high in the hours after your rescue. Whatever he said, whatever you said, probably meant nothing at all. Why don't you call him? Tell him you want to see him."

"Because I don't want to see him."

"Liar, liar, pants on fire . . ."

Jeanie smiled.

"Seriously, you have to pull out of this depression you're in. The way you have yourself locked up so tight, you might just as well have stayed in that cave."

"He said that's what I am."

Sharon shot her a look. "What does that mean?"

"He said I'm trapped in a cave of my own making. That I'm all locked up in my own fear of being trapped, just as surely as I was locked up in Grandpa's closet."

"Why did he say that? What is it he thinks you're afraid of?"

"He wanted me to marry him."

Sharon stared. "And you wouldn't? It's obvious that you're madly in love with him, and he with you. So why ever did you turn him down?"

"He's not in love with me. He doesn't believe in love. He wants to marry me so that women will stop chasing him and start chasing Rolph."

Sharon threw back her head and laughed, the clear, tinkling sound rising up to bounce back off the rough beams that formed the ceiling of the living room. "Of all the crazy rationales for a proposal! And are you really so dumb as to think that's his real reason? Jeanie, no man would marry to give his brother a clear run at the field. If he told you that, it's because he's scared to death to admit he loves you."

"He told me that the second time I'd ever seen him. He proposed to me after knowing me for roughly two hours."

Sharon's jet-black eyes widened. "No kidding! The guy must really have been smitten. Love at first sight." She sighed and smiled happily like the true romantic she was.

"Sharon! I just told you. He was nothing of the sort. He wants to give Rolph a break. Rolph actually suggested that it would help if Max took himself out of circulation."

"Listen, babe, you met Rolph. The guy's gorgeous. He can't be having trouble attracting women, no matter how handsome his brother is. Surely, there are enough women to go around that they could both take their pick." She paused and shook her head in disgust. "And Max McKenzie, whether he knows it or not, has taken his pick. And you, my beloved little sister, are it. Now, are you going to spend the rest of your life sitting here sulking, or are you going to get off your duff and go after what you know, deep down, is the only man in the world for you?"

"He'll try to control me."

"Sure he will. Don't let him."

"He'll order me around, like Ellis ordered you around. He'll turn me into a—" Her gaze fell and she stared at her hands linked in her lap. She rubbed them together. Ever since she'd come home from hospital, her hands had been so cold, she thought they'd never get warm again.

"Ahh, so that's it." Sharon got off her chair and knelt before Jeanie, taking the thin, cold hands in her own warm ones. "Listen, babe. You never did understand about me and Ellis, did you? You saw the bad parts but never the good ones."

Jeanie lifted a skeptical brow. "There were good parts to your marriage?"

"Yes. But you weren't there then. You were at college. The first few years were wonderful. When I became more . . . important than he was, more famous, he couldn't stand that, Jeanie. That was when the bad stuff started. I'm not excusing him. I know he was a bastard of the first degree. I knew I should have left him the first time he hurt me, but I loved him, and I told myself that he'd just lost his temper. By the time I realized that he was losing his temper too often, it was too late. I was caught in that terrible downward spiral that battered wives get caught in."

"He took away your self-respect. He stole your ability to compose! He ate up your soul, Sharon!"

"Yes, in a way, I guess he did. But that, Jeanie, was my fault. I let him do that to me." She paused thoughtfully for several moments. "I like to think I would have been able to pull myself out of it somehow, got the help I needed, but I'll never know, will I? Because he was the one who left me in the end."

"And still you never regained what he'd taken from you. You don't make music anymore. How could I risk letting some man destroy my soul that way, after seeing what happened to you?"

"No!" Sharon got to her feet, the lamplight turning her black hair almost blue as she paced angrily away, then back toward her sister. "I won't permit that, Jeanie! If you're letting my experiences color what you feel about marriage, stop right now. Marriage is a fine and wonderful thing between the right people. Ellis and I were the wrong people. That's all. Pure and simple."

"Last year, when you told me that you wished you could get over being afraid of men, because you'd like to marry again, have a father for the kids, I thought you were crazy, Sharon. How could you want another man in your life after what Ellis did to you?"

Sharon returned to crouch before her troubled younger sister. "Because, my dearest, all men are not like Ellis. I know that somewhere out there, there's the right man for me. A man who can love me for what I am, who I am, and accept my limitations."

Jeanie leaned forward and put her head on Sharon's shoulder. "You don't have any, Sharon. If only you could see that. You really have no limitations at all in spite of what Ellis made you believe. You *are* more talented than he is. It was no fluke you became more famous. It wasn't just because you were a woman and the music world needed a token woman composer. Oh, Sharon, I want so much for you to be like you were before."

Lifting her head, she said, "Just once, will you play for me, will you at least try?"

Sharon glanced over at where her harp stood in the corner. For a moment, Jeanie thought she might get up and walk over to it, but then she shook her head.

"How 'bout this," she said, her throat working. "I'll play at your wedding, little sister. As long as you go and get that man who is the right one for you."

On the long and tortuous drive, Jeanie began to realize that the McKenzie brothers, in spite of their physical differences, were really very much alike. Rolph might have been a little gentler in nature, but he had the same wry, puckish sense of humor, and even sounded like Max when he laughed. And he laughed a lot on that long drive.

"Make sure you stop and let me out before we get close enough for him to hear the truck," she said for the third time, glimpsing the roof of the cabin and the glint from the bubble of the helicopter perched on its pad nearby. "I don't want him taking off until I've had a chance to talk to him."

"If I had my way, I'd drive right up to the cabin, jump out, and smash his tail rotor, leaving you two here alone until you talked some sense into him."

Rolph gave her a squeeze as he pulled the four-by-four to a stop. "I'm just glad one of you began to see reason. A month of this dough-headedness of his was all the family could stand. If Freda hadn't threatened to quit, I don't think we could have got him up here to pull himself out of his funk and decide one way or another what he was going to do about you."

"There you go, kiddo." He handed her her back-pack and gave her a little salute. "On your way. If I see that chopper take off within the next ten minutes, I'll come down to the cabin for you. After that, I'm gone."

"The chopper will not take off," she said. "When it comes to handling heroes, I know exactly what to do."

But for all her bold words, Jeanie was shaking as she walked along the track and came in sight of the cabin. The door was closed. Almost on tip-toe, she bypassed the cabin, went to the helicop-ter, and did what Rolph had laughingly suggested she could do. Then she walked up the three steps to the porch and lifted the hand-made wooden latch of the door. Its hinges squeaked as she pushed it open. The two windows, one looking out over the lake, the other into the forest, were undraped. Through the one in the front, she saw Max a hundred feet below, fishing from a canoe.

Should she wait? Should she call him? She trembled with joy at the sight of him. No matter what the outcome of this visit was, she had to see him.

On the dumpy looking leather couch lay a golden trumpet. Picking it up, she firmed her lips, pressed them against it, and placed her fin-gers on the keys. Gently, she coaxed long, low tones from it until she had its measure. Then, opening the door, she stepped out onto the nar-row porch and lifted the horn high into the glint-ing December sun.

Into the wind she played for him. Into the mountains the echos carried and returned, notes high and clear and throbbing and pure. Over the water her message flew and floated, and he looked up.

Il Silenzio! He dropped his rod over the side, picked up his paddle, and shot that canoe to the shore. He was out of breath when he reached the porch. Gently taking the trumpet from her lips, he replaced it with his mouth.

"You didn't tell me you could play," he said when he could speak.

"You didn't ask."

"You're better than I am."

She shrugged. "I took lessons for years. All the Leslies are musically talented. Do you care?"

"Not a bit. I dig better than you do."

She smiled. "That's true."

"Do you care that I'm bigger and stronger?"

Her smile faded, her face becoming serious. "Not a bit. I love better than you do."

He drew a deep breath and let it out in a rush; his eyes showed a hint of fear, but he said, "No you don't. I love you, Jeanie. With all my heart and soul, I do. But, oh, Lord, it scares me to feel this way!"

"Yes, I know you love me. That's why I'm here. And I know it scares you too."

He looked at her, his blue eyes full of questions. "You know I love you? But how can you? I only knew it myself the minute I heard that horn and looked up and saw you all golden in the sun, calling to me with music we both love."

"Max . . . Max. Would you have gone flinging yourself into a collapsing tunnel for anyone else?"

He smiled and shook his head. "No. Only for you. If it had been anyone else, I'd have done the smart thing and got the hell out and gone for help. Only I couldn't stand the thought of your being alone in there, afraid, maybe hurt."

"So. You see? That's love, Max."

She felt his nod against her face, heard his whisper near her ear. "I guess it is."

"Please don't be scared of loving me, my love." She trembled as she leaned back in his arms and met his seeking gaze. "I'll help you deal with that, if you'll do for me what you did before—talk to me, keep me calm, show me that the cages I fear are all in my mind. Max, I've come to ask if you still want to marry me."

His sigh was ragged and his kiss was deep, telling her of his love the way no words ever could. "I'll always want to marry you," he said, "and I'll always want to be married to you. When? When can we make it official?"

She laughed and buried her face against his chest. "That depends. How long will it take your brother to drive from here to Victoria and back to bring in a bunch of aviation fuel? I'm afraid, Mr. McKenzie, your helicopter's out of gas."

He stared at her. "How in the hell did that happen?"

Impishly, she held up the tool she'd had tucked in her jacket pocket. "Rolph told me about a little plug at the bottom of the tank. I wasn't sure you were going to give me much chance to talk to you and . . . well . . ."

"I'm not," he said with a growl, picking her up and carrying her inside the cabin. It was cold that high in the mountains, even in the sun. And the building clouds portended snow. Rolph might not be back for a long time.

"I don't want talk. I want action!" He carried her up the stairs to the loft bed where the warmth of the wood heater below wafted up over them. He laid her down, taking off her down coat, her sweater, and her shoes and socks and jeans.

"You," he said, "should not be running around without underwear in the middle of December. You might catch cold."

"You might catch more than cold if you don't hurry up," she told him.

"What might I catch?"

"A bust in the mouth, mister."

He didn't mind a bit.

It was still night when they awoke. "Your head's on my pillow," Max said, rolling over to look at her in the glow of an oil lamp.

"I noticed. Want me to move it?"

"Never." They shared a smile of joy.

"Max? You know what Jason found out about that cave at school?"

"Hmm? What?" He didn't much care. He was busy sliding the thick duvet back very, very slowly, making discoveries as he went.

"A kid in seventh grade set it up. He was going to invite his girlfriend there. He wrote her a note, but someone else got hold of it, and it was all over the school in no time at all. He was too embarrassed to go back and get his stuff."

"Hmm! I see. Sort of like wanting to take her out behind the firestation or down to the marina to his dad's boat?"

"Guess so. Naughty, huh?"

"Only if she agreed to do it."

"Double standard already, Mr. McKenzie?"

"Double standards aren't for grown-ups."

He rolled over and scribbled on the notepad he

always kept at his bedside, then handed her the note.

She read it aloud. "Dear Jeanie. I love you. Wanna go down to my couch and do it?"

She blinked at him innocently. "What does 'do it' mean?"

With a lascivious grin he picked her up and carried her down to the couch. "Just you lie back right there," he said, "and let ol' Maxie show you."

She opened her arms to him and murmured, "What a hero!" And within the sounds of their mingled laughter, Jeanie distinctly heard the tinkling music of golden bangles. Looking over Max's shoulder, she winked and said silently, *Thanks, Grandma Margaret. Thanks for everything.*

THE EDITOR'S CORNER

In publishing a series such as LOVESWEPT we couldn't function without timetables, schedules, deadlines. It seems we're always working toward one, only to reach it then strive for another. I mention the topic because many of you write and ask us questions about the way we work and about how and when certain books are published. Just consider this Editor's Corner as an example. I'm writing this in early April, previewing our October books, which will run in our September books, which will be on sale in August. The books you're reading about were scheduled for publication at least nine months earlier and were probably written more than a year before they reach your hands! Six books a month means seventy-two a year, and we're into our seventh year of publication. That's a lot of books and a lot of information to try to keep up with. Amazingly, we do keep up—and so do our authors. We enjoy providing you with the answer to a question about a particular book or author or character. Your letters mean a lot to us.

In our ongoing effort to extend the person-to-person philosophy of LOVESWEPT, we are setting up a 900 number through which you can learn what's new—and what's old—with your favorite authors! Next month's Editor's Corner will have the full details for you.

Kay Hooper's most successful series for us to date has been her *Once Upon a Time . . .* novels. These modern-day fairy tales have struck a chord with you, the readers, and your enjoyment of the books has delighted and inspired Kay. Her next in this series is LOVESWEPT #426, **THE LADY AND THE LION,** and it's one of Kay's sizzlers. Keith Donovan and Erin Prentice first speak to each other from their adjacent hotel balconies, sharing secrets and desperate murmurings in the dark. Kay creates a moody, evocative, emotionally charged atmosphere in which these two kindred spirits fall in love before they ever meet. But when they finally do set eyes on each other, they know without having to speak that they've found their destinies. This wonderful story will bring out the true romantic in all of you!

We take you from fairy tales to fairyland this month! Our next LOVESWEPT, #427, **SATIN SHEETS AND STRAWBERRIES** by Marcia Evanick, features a golden-haired nymph of a heroine named Kelli SantaFe. Hero Logan Sinclair does a double take when he arrives at what looks like Snow White's cottage in search of his aunt and uncle—and finds a bewitching woman dressed as a fairy. Kelli runs her business from her home and at first resents Logan's interference and the tug-of-war he wages for his relatives, whom she'd taken in and treated like the family

(continued)

she'd always wanted. Logan is infuriated by her stubbornness, yet intrigued by the woman who makes him feel as though his feet barely touch the ground. Kelli falls hard for Logan, who can laugh at himself and rescue damsels in distress, but who has the power to shatter her happiness. You'll find you're enchanted by the time Kelli and Logan discover how to weave their dreams together!

All of us feel proud and excited whenever we publish a new author in the line. The lady whose work we're introducing you to next month is a talented, hardworking mother of five who strongly believes in the importance of sprinkling each day with a little romance. We think Olivia Rupprecht does just that with **BAD BOY OF NEW ORLEANS,** LOVESWEPT #428. I don't know about you, but some of my all-time favorite romances involve characters who reunite after years apart. I find these stories often epitomize the meaning of true love. Well, in **BAD BOY OF NEW ORLEANS** Olivia reunites two people whose maddening hunger for each other has only deepened with time. Hero Chance Renault can still make Micah Sinclair tremble, can still make her burn for his touch and cry out for the man who had loved her first. But over time they've both changed, and a lot stands between them. Micah feels she must prove she can survive on her own, while Chance insists she belongs to him body and soul. Their journey toward happiness together is one you won't want to miss!

Joan Elliott Pickart never ceases to amaze me with the way she is able to provide us with winning romance after winning romance. She's truly a phenomenon, and we're pleased and honored to bring you her next LOVESWEPT, #429, **STORMING THE CASTLE**. While reunited lovers have their own sets of problems to overcome, when two very different people find themselves falling in love, their long-held beliefs, values, and lifestyles become an issue. In **STORMING THE CASTLE,** Dr. Maggie O'Leary finds her new hunk of a neighbor, James-Steven Payton, to be a free spirit, elusive as the wind and just as irresistible. Leave it to him to choose the unconventional over the customary way of doing things. But Maggie grew up with a father who was much the same, whose devil-may-care ways often brought heartache. James-Steven longs to see the carefree side of Maggie, and he sets out to get her to smell the flowers and to build sand castles without worrying that the tide will wash them away. Though Maggie longs to join her heart to his, she knows they must first find a common ground. Joan handles this tender story beautifully. It's a real heart-warmer!

One author who always delivers a fresh, innovative story is Mary Kay McComas. Each of her LOVESWEPTs is unique and imaginative—never the same old thing! In **FAVORS,** LOVESWEPT #430, Mary Kay has once again let her creative juices flow, and

(continued)

the result is a story unlike any other. Drawing on her strength in developing characters you come to know intimately and completely, Mary Kay serves up a romance filled with emotion and chock full of fun. Her tongue-in-cheek portrayal of several secondary characters will have you giggling, and her surprise ending will add the finishing touch to your enjoyment of the story. When agent Ian Walker is asked to protect a witness as a favor to his boss, he considers the job no more appealing than baby-sitting—until he meets Trudy Babbitt, alias Pollyanna. The woman infuriates him by refusing to believe she's in danger—and ignites feelings in him he'd thought were long dead. Trudy sees beneath Ian's crusty exterior and knows she can transform him with her love. But first they have to deal with the reality of their situation. I don't want to give away too much, so I'll just suggest you keep in mind while reading **FAVORS** that nothing is exactly as it seems. Crafty Mary Kay pulls a few aces from her sleeve!

One of your favorite authors—and ours—Billie Green returns to our lineup next month with **SWEET AND WILDE, #431**. Billie has always been able to capture that indefinable quality that makes a LOVESWEPT romance special. In her latest for us, she throws together an unlikely pair of lovers, privileged Alyson Wilde and streetwise Sid Sweet and sends them on an incredible adventure. You might wonder what a blue-blooded lady could have in common with a bail bondsman and pawnshop owner, but Billie manages to keep her characters more than a little bit interested in each other. When thirteen-year-old Lenny, who is Alyson's ward, insists that his friend Sid Sweet is a great guy and role model, Alyson decides she has to meet the tough-talking man for herself. And cynical Sid worries that Good Samaritan Alyson has taken Lenny on only as her latest "project." With Lenny's best interests at heart, they go with him in search of his past and end up discovering their own remarkable future—one filled with a real love that is better than any of their fantasies.

Be sure to pick up all six books next month. They're all keepers!

Sincerely,

Susann Brailey

Susann Brailey
Editor
LOVESWEPT
Bantam Books
666 Fifth Avenue
New York, NY 10103

FAN OF THE MONTH

Sandra Beattie

How did I come to be such a fan of LOVESWEPT romances? It was by accident, really. My husband was in the Australian Navy and we were moving once again to another state. I wanted some books to read while we stayed in the motel, so I went to a second-hand bookstore in search of some Silhouette romances. I spotted some books I hadn't seen before, and after reading the back covers I decided to buy two. I asked the saleslady to set the rest aside in case I wanted them later. I read both books that night and was hooked. I raced back to the store the next day and bought the rest. I've been a fan of LOVESWEPT ever since.

My favorite authors are Sandra Brown, Kay Hooper, Iris Johansen, Fayrene Preston, Joan Elliott Pickart, and Mary Kay McComas. The thing I like about LOVESWEPT heroes is that they are not always rich and handsome men, but some are struggling like us. I cry and laugh with the people in the books. Sometimes I become them and feel everything that they feel. The love scenes are just so romantic that they take my breath away. But then some of them are funny as well.

I'm thirty-four years old, the mother of three children. I love rock and roll, watching old movies, and snuggling up to my husband on cold, rainy nights. If there is one thing I can pass on to other readers, it is that you can't let everything get you down. When I feel depressed, I pick up a LOVESWEPT and curl up in a chair for a while and just forget about everything. Then when I get up again, the world doesn't look so bad anymore. Try it, it really works!